"Turn around, [   ]t you look like fr[   ]d.

"What?"

"So I can figure out which style of jeans to bring into the dressing room for you. Come on, men do this to women all the time."

He accepted defeat and turned aroud. "Well?"

She eyed his firm, muscular body with an appraising gaze. "Definitely tight fit, sculpted bottom."

He laughed. "Just get me the jeans."

When she'd picked out an armful of clothes, she stood at the curtain of his dressing room. "Damien, I've brought—"

He reached out a hand and yanked her into the room with him, then pulled the curtain closed.

"What are you doing, Damien?" she asked with breathless laughter. He stood there dressed only in black briefs. He grabbed the clothes from her and tossed them aside.

"I'm about to get the kiss I've needed for the last three hours," he said, pushing her back against the mirror with his body. The contact was electric. He pressed his lips against hers with a hunger that destroyed whatever defenses she might have mustered. She gave in to the passion he awakened in her, because there was nothing else she could do. There was no holding back the tide of her emotions, the wildfire of her need . . . and his. . . .

WHAT ARE *LOVESWEPT* ROMANCES?

They are stories of true romance and touching emotion. We believe those two very important ingredients are constants in our highly sensual and very believable stories in the *LOVESWEPT* line. Our goal is to give you, the reader, stories of consistently high quality that may sometimes make you laugh, sometimes make you cry, but are always fresh and creative and contain many delightful surprises within their pages.

Most romance fans read an enormous number of books. Those they truly love, they keep. Others may be traded with friends and soon forgotten. We hope that each *LOVESWEPT* romance will be a treasure—a "keeper." We will always try to publish

LOVE STORIES YOU'LL NEVER FORGET
BY AUTHORS YOU'LL ALWAYS REMEMBER

The Editors

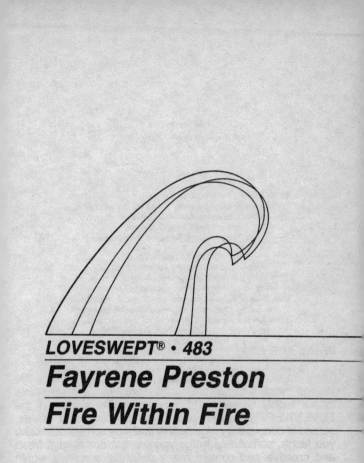

LOVESWEPT® • 483

Fayrene Preston

Fire Within Fire

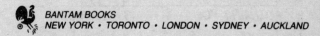

BANTAM BOOKS
NEW YORK • TORONTO • LONDON • SYDNEY • AUCKLAND

FIRE WITHIN FIRE
A Bantam Book / July 1991

*If you would be interested in receiving protective vinyl
covers for your Loveswept books, please write to this address
for information:*

> *Loveswept*
> *Bantam Books*
> *P.O. Box 985*
> *Hicksville, NY 11802*

ISBN 0-553-44148-5

To Murray McCord,
For the houseboats
and
To his lovely lady, Jennifer
For her constant support and friendship.

FIRE WITHIN FIRE

One

Ginnie Summers jogged along the northern California beach toward the inn. *Would he be there again?* she wondered. For the past five days the stranger had sat there alone on the private upper balcony of the inn each morning and watched her. Even from a distance she could discern the brooding intensity with which he regarded her.

The balcony he sat on was used exclusively by the owner of the inn and his guests. She supposed the stranger was one of Max Hayden's friends or guests. And the titillating mystery of him had had her waking up much earlier in the morning these past few days.

She loved her dawn runs when no one else was awake but her. The ocean and the seabirds provided natural music, and the beginning of a brand new day provided unending possibilities. She believed in music. She believed in unending possibilities. And for some reason that she couldn't explain, she believed she would see the stranger again in just a few moments. Dark excitement rose in her.

As she approached the inn, her pulse jumped, then accelerated. *He was there*, waiting for her, a forceful figure in the light of the rising sun, enigmatic, with a hint of danger. She slowed.

This morning, he seemed to be sitting closer than usual to the railing. She could see the thickness of his light brown hair, and the powerful line of his broad shoulders, and the muscled form of his body. And as she drew even with him, he leaned forward and clutched the railing with a strength and a tension that positively electrified her. His gaze was so searing, she was surprised she had any skin left on her body. She was shaken, unnerved, and flushed with . . . Arousal? It didn't make sense, but there seemed to be a chain of heat that linked them.

Damien Averone watched her come toward him from beneath hooded eyes. Nerves throughout his body prickled and fired in response, and he softly cursed with disgust at himself. Her effect on him was ridiculous, he thought, even as he kept his gaze glued to her.

She ran barefoot, in leggings topped by an oversized sweater that came down past her hips. Her legs were extraordinarily long and slender, and just looking at them made his stomach knot. Her hair swayed from side to side, a disordered mass of reddish-brown waves that his fingers itched to touch.

Where did she come from? he wondered. How far did she have to run each day before she reached the inn? And, more important, when she woke in the morning and reached for the leggings and sweater, did she leave someone in bed who waited for her to return to him?

He cursed again. During the day when he was conducting business meetings. During the night when he tried to sleep. Dammit, she was *haunting* him. Over and over the image of the breathtakingly sexy long-legged beauty covering the sand in a graceful, gazellelike lope came to him.

She set fire to his blood, she interfered with his thoughts.

Dammit, he needed to put her out of his mind.

She had disappeared from his view now, but he knew from previous mornings that she ran as far as a sand dune about half a mile down the beach, turned, and came back.

Behind him, he heard Max walk onto the balcony. Damien glanced around at him. "Did you see the woman who just jogged past here?"

Max plopped his solid, warm-up–clad length down in the chair next to Damien's and squinted his eyes against the glint the rising sun was creating on the water. "I don't see well before ten A.M. anymore. If you'll remember, I'm retired from Wall Street, and that includes those hellish early hours I used to start at. Actually, now that I think about it, I need to go back to bed. It may be nine A.M. back in New York, but it's the break of dawn here."

"I don't give a damn what time it is, Max. I want to know if you saw her."

Max yawned. "No."

"Well, apparently she jogs by here every morning.

She has long reddish-brown hair, and legs that seem to start at about her shoulders. Does that sound familiar to you? Do you have any idea who she could be?" His gaze automatically returned to the distant point down the beach where he would catch sight of her again.

"Yes."

His head swung around. "Yes?"

Max began whistling a pop hit.

Damien brought his teeth together with an impatient snap. "Are you going to make me ask?"

With a grin Max slouched down in his chair and stretched his legs out in front of him. "I've had a bet with myself on how long it would take you."

Damien fixed his friend with a scathing look that would have intimidated any other man. "I had no idea you'd become so provincial since you moved out here. It doesn't seem to take much at all to amuse you."

"Maybe," Max said cheerfully. "But I know who she is, and you don't."

Damien sighed. He knew from years of experience that very few people ever won an argument with Max. "Okay, okay, I'm asking. Who is she?"

"Her name's Ginnie Summers. She lives on a houseboat a few miles down the beach, and teaches music to private students."

"Does she live alone?"

"Yes."

The magnitude of the relief he felt gave him pause. After all, it wasn't as if he were going to do anything about her. He pursued companies, not women. "Music," he said thoughtfully. "One night I heard the faint sounds of a guitar being played. I didn't know where it was coming from. Do you think it was Ginnie Summers?"

Max shrugged. "I don't know who else it could have been, and I guess if she was down on the beach and the wind was right . . ."

Damien's heart hammered as she reappeared, coming back toward him.

"Why don't you go down and introduce yourself?" Max asked.

He shook his head with more force than necessary. "Relationships aren't my thing. You know that."

"Who said anything about a relationship? Just meet her. Ask her to dinner tonight. You'd have a pleasant evening. Then tomorrow you could get in your plane and fly back to New York as scheduled. Better yet, let's take off some place. I'll fly. How does Hong Kong strike you? I haven't been there in a couple of years—"

"No."

"No to Hong Kong? Okay, well, how about Australia? We could get in some serious deep-sea fishing. We could even try some surfing. I've always wanted to surf."

"No to everything you just said." He couldn't imagine having anything as insipid as a *pleasant* evening with Ginnie Summers. Exhilarating, yes. Passionate, yes. Wild, definitely. His thoughts took a sharp turn. He suddenly realized she reminded him of the music he had heard. Lovely, passionate, haunting . . .

As she drew even with them, Max lifted his hand and called, " 'Morning, Ginnie."

Her overly wide, decidedly sensual mouth spread into a smile. She waved and ran on.

Fascination drummed through Damien's bloodstream. And he continued to remain irritated and unsettled.

Damien walked away from the inn, his long, muscular legs striding swiftly over the sand of the moonlit beach. The warm northern California night called for a leisurely stroll, but he never did anything in a leisurely way. The restlessness was always with him. He hated it; he accepted it. It ran beneath his skin like live electrical wires, pulsing, driving him—and tonight he was even more driven.

Tonight he was in search of *her.* Ginnie Summers.

Ginnie Summers. Lovely name, he thought. Mind-blowing woman.

All evening, while concluding a meeting with two of his executives who were handling a takeover, the thought of her had been tiny, fiery thorns pricking at him. In desperation he'd taken several deep breaths, had a drink of water, and got up and paced the room. Then, without warning, the control he'd been exercising over himself had snapped. Dammit, what he was doing was totally crazy, traipsing down a beach in search of someone he'd seen only for a short period on each of five days.

Dark gray gossamer wisps of clouds drifted across a black, star-strewn sky. The silver light of the full moon made the ocean shimmer like silk and the sand gleam like gold. It was odd, but he didn't think he had ever walked on a beach at night before. There was a sense of primeval majesty about it; there was also a sense of unreality.

If he saw her again and talked with her, he was sure he would be rid of his infatuation for her. Then, first thing in the morning, he would fly back to New York.

He came to a stop as the faint sound of music reached his ears. Guitar music, soft and lilting. *It was she.* He glanced around, but the beach was deserted. The nearest structure of any kind, the inn, was a mile behind him. The road was up the bluff and half a mile to his left, and he could see no boats on the ocean to his right. Where was she?

He continued on. The music grew louder and stronger, developing into an entrancing rhythm and melody that combined intense sensuality and a vivid energy. His steps quickened. It sounded like nothing he had ever known before—melodic phrases that wove together and produced a song both evocatively beautiful and deeply passionate.

Then he saw her, and any hope he'd harbored for a cure for his fascination disappeared. She was sitting on a rock at the water's edge, cradling a guitar against her as if it were an extension of her body and playing it as he had never heard anyone play.

The moon trailed its light over her. She could have materialized out of a moonbeam or ocean spray. But he knew better. She was flesh and blood, all long legs and flyaway hair, and capable of making him desire her before he had even known her name.

He eased closer, until he was within a step or two of her.

She was bent over the guitar, her eyes closed, her hair a mass of waves that fell at an angle across her face. She was barefoot and wearing an over-sized cable-knit sweater and a skirt made of something filmy that drifted on the night's breeze. Moonlight pearlized her skin and kissed her full lips. A sudden urge came over him to kiss those lips.

But he couldn't seem to do anything other than stand there, stare at her, listen to the music, and wonder.

Where was the power coming from? The passion? How could such frail-looking hands and delicate wrists force such heartrendingly beautiful music from a simple wood-and-string guitar? He had to find out. He had to get to know her. He had to kiss her. She had insinuated herself into his bloodstream, and he didn't know how to purge himself.

The music was building, piling emotion and notes, one onto the other, growing in tempo and mood until his breath was in his throat. He was listening to something very personal, he realized. The music was the woman. Unknowingly, she was pouring herself into him. It was as if she were making an exotic and ultra-erotic kind of love to him.

Stirred, compelled, he had no choice but to listen. And as he did, the music she was making flowed into his heart where there was always a longing, into his gut where there was always an emptiness, into his soul where there was always a restlessness.

He was excited; he was soothed.

Waves spilled onto the sand and spread a luminescent foam around the rock upon which she sat, but Ginnie was aware of nothing but her music. Through her fingers she talked to the well-loved instrument, and it in turn relayed what she was feeling out over the sea. Only at times like this when she was all alone did she allow herself the freedom to open herself completely and take her music to the edge and then beyond. Her heart was her composer.

She listened as the notes lingered in the air, then gradually dispersed on the gentle breeze. She stayed as she was, bent over the guitar, still feeling the music reverberate within her and savoring the exhilaration.

Then slowly she lifted her head and opened her eyes and saw him.

Him!

She couldn't mistake the intensity he emitted, or the tension in the lean, muscled lines of his body, or the penetrating intensity of his eyes.

Then she received her second shock. The expression on his ruggedly handsome face seemed to convey a passion so similar to what she had been putting into her music that she shivered. Without her being aware of it, he had been in her mind when she had been playing. In fact, *he* was the music she had been playing, the embodiment of all the pent-up longing and desire that was within her.

"I don't think I've ever heard anything more

beautiful," he said huskily, and saw her eyes widen. In the moonlight he couldn't make out their exact color, but they were light, and he knew without knowing that they held secret dreams. "Don't be afraid."

His voice sounded like silk over granite, she thought, inwardly scrambling to cope with her physical reaction. Quite simply, her heart felt as though it would burst.

For days she had wondered and fantasized about him. Now he was here, dressed in a business suit. On the beach. At midnight. And confirming every single one of her impressions. He was dangerously sexy, with a hard, powerful body and eyes that generated a searing heat. And he was exuding a sensuality that pulled on her as strongly as the moon's pull on the tide.

"You're a man I should be afraid of, aren't you?" she asked.

Her question made him smile. He had meant to reassure her about physical peril. But now she was referring to another kind of peril. "I think so."

Transfixed, she watched as moon shadows played over the angles and planes of his strong face, highlighting, delineating. By listening to her play, he had invaded her mind and her heart without her permission. He had been privy to her most intimate feelings, feelings of which he had been a part. In a way it was an invasion of the most sensual kind. She was torn, wanting to surrender to the attraction, but knowing she should fight against it.

With an agitated sweep of her hand she flicked a wavy mass of hair behind her shoulder. "If I had known you were there, I would have stopped playing." She stood and rested the guitar against the rock.

He slipped his hands into his pockets. "That would have been a shame, because I loved what I heard."

She looked up at him through the thickness of her lashes. "You did?"

He nodded, noting the uncertainty in her voice. "I'm sure you must be used to compliments about your playing, but I'd like to tell you anyway. You play beautifully, and with more passion than I've ever heard." He paused. "My name is Damien Averone. I'm a friend of Max's."

"I'm Ginnie"—she lifted one shoulder and let it fall—"I'm sure Max told you." She was getting over the shock that he had heard her play. Next she had to get over the shock that the attraction she had felt for him all week was even more potent now that they were separated by only a foot of moonlight.

"I know your name," he murmured. "I also know you're the most passionate woman I've ever met."

A quiver of warm surprise ran through her. "You can't know that."

"Think about it and you'll realize I can. The song you played was you, and somehow it went into me and touched all sorts of places. How did you do that?"

Disturbed, aroused, she wrapped her arms around herself. "It wasn't intentional."

"Which made it all the more effective." He paused. "How else do you expend your passion?"

It was dangerous to be talking about passion

with a stranger on the beach at midnight. But how could she turn and walk away from a man who had heard her most intimate feelings and seemed to understand? "I don't need to do anything else."

"Yes, you do," he said softly. "I heard the longing in your music."

Longing had been there, plus so much more, she thought. And he had heard it all. But then, in a way, she realized, it was her own fault. He had been in her thoughts as she played. She had practically summoned him to her with her music. *Good heavens.*

"Max said you live on a houseboat nearby?"

"Yes."

"You live on the water, you run by the water. And you make music at the water's edge . . . and at night. I find that really interesting."

"You do? Why?"

He reached out and pressed a finger to her bottom lip, exerting just enough pressure to pull the lip out so that he could skim his finger inside to the moist softness. Then he put the same finger into his mouth.

Heat shot through her, and her legs weakened. "What are you doing?"

"I wanted to find out what you tasted like."

His lips curved upward, humorously, sexily. Incapable of doing anything else, she followed the movement with her eyes.

He went on, "You see, I had a little sea-siren theory going, and I almost believed you'd taste cool and salty, like the water. But you don't. You taste warm and sweet, like honey." He shrugged. "My sea-siren theory just went out the window."

"Gee, I'm sorry about that." Her tone was light-hearted, but inwardly she was dismayed at the desire growing within her. Once again her gaze went to his lips. They looked firm and sculpted with a fullness that seemed to her sensuous beyond belief. What would it be like . . . ?

"Oh, it's all right. You fit the definition of a siren anyway. A temptingly beautiful woman. Insidiously seductive. Siren describes you to a T." His smile slowly faded. "And I definitely have to have more of your taste." Gazing deeply into her eyes, he reached out and closed his hands around her upper arms. "You know we've got to kiss, don't you?"

She wasn't sure if she said yes. But in her mind she heard the word over and over again. Then, slowly, he drew her into his arms.

Given that they'd met only minutes before, their kiss should have been tentative and uncertain, Ginnie thought, a dreamlike haze descending around her. But when their mouths met, it was as if they had known and wanted each other for a long time. And in a way, she supposed they had.

The pressure of his lips was hard and demanding, and her lips parted immediately, welcoming his tongue and the burning sensuality that came with it. And even the wild, tumultuous feelings the kiss created seemed to her like old friends, as if the heat and the searing sweetness had been in her all along, waiting for this moment to surface. The joining of their lips was something that had to be.

He changed the angle of his head and took her mouth again. His hungry kiss stripped away incidental emotion, leaving only the bare bones of shattering passion. A fire scorched through her, taking her strength with it.

"This is crazy," he muttered gruffly, skimming his mouth down her neck and back up again. "But I've never known anything that felt so right."

Her stomach clenched, and she had to agree with him. Every bone in her body ached for him, and strangely, at this moment, she couldn't remember a time when they hadn't. But . . .

The tip of a breaking wave climbed up the beach, reaching to her bare feet, conveying a sudden coolness that went straight through her. It was all too much, too fast, too soon, too irrational.

"No . . ." The word came out on a breathless whisper.

But he heard. Reluctantly, gradually, he pulled away. But he couldn't keep from touching her. He ran his hand over her hair, smoothing the wild curls. "What is it?"

"I have to leave now."

"Not yet." His voice sounded raw and rough-edged. It matched the way he felt inside.

She took a step away from him, and he panicked. "Wait, don't go yet. First I have to tell you something."

She eyed him warily, not because she didn't trust him, but because she didn't trust herself. "What?"

"When you were playing, I felt as if you were making love to me. When you finished and raised your head, you had the most rapturous look on your face. It was a look I'll never forget. It was also a look I want to see again."

What could she say? How could she explain that he had been a part of the music she had played? It didn't even make sense to her. She grabbed up her guitar, whirled, and ran down the beach, into the night.

Damien watched until the darkness swallowed her. Then he turned and walked slowly back to the inn, an expression of determination on his face.

Damien sent an annoyed look across the breakfast table to Max. Clad in sweats, he was devoting an inordinate amount of time and attention to sectioning his grapefruit. "Will you forget the damned grapefruit and give me an answer? How well do you know her?"

Damien's impatience provoked a twinkle in Max's dark blue eyes. "In case you haven't noticed, this isn't New York City. It's a small town. Everyone knows practically everyone."

"You've already told me you know her. What I'm asking is, how *well* do you know her?" He was unsuccessful at keeping the jealousy out of his voice, but he offered no apologies. After he and Max had graduated from the Wharton School of Finance and Commerce, they had lived next door to each other in New York, and he remembered all too well the number of Max's conquests. And the thought of Max or of any other man making love to Ginnie had him ready to destroy something . . . or someone.

Max grinned knowingly. "There's no reason to give me that trademark Averone killer stare. Ginnie's never been more than a casual acquaintance.

She's lived in town a couple of years, and I see her around."

"Does she ever come here to eat?"

"Occasionally. And to answer your next question, she usually comes in alone."

"Usually?"

Max shook his head in disbelief. "I don't think I've ever seen you like this. What happened last night, anyway?"

"None of your damned business."

"Now I *know* I've never seen you like this."

He could feel what little was left of his patience fraying. He adjusted the French cuff of his shirt with a jerk. "What I want to know is if she's seeing anyone on a regular basis. Dammit, I want to know if she's *involved* with someone."

"Not that I know of. More coffee?"

"No." Damien reached into the pocket of his suit for a pen and pad. "How do I get to her houseboat?"

"It's moored down at the marina. I'm not sure exactly where or which one."

"I can't thank you enough. You're a regular fount of information."

"Yeah, well, there is one more thing I need to tell you."

"If you're about to tell me there's someone in her life—"

"There is, but not in the way you mean. It's her stepfather. He drives up from San Francisco every once in a while, and they come here for dinner."

"So?"

The twinkle in Max's eyes became even more pronounced. "Her stepfather is Nathan Camden, who just happens to be head of the company you are taking over."

Damien replaced the pen and pad in his inside jacket pocket. "I hope she has stock in the company, because it's about to double in value."

Max eyed him curiously. "Are you going to tell her what you're doing?"

Damien leaned back in the chair and glanced out over the ocean. The day was sparkling clear, and the ocean held a tint of blue. His restlessness was back again. He needed to find her, be with her, touch her, taste her. . . . "She's completely separate from my business."

Max grinned. "There was a time when I understood that kind of logic."

Damien cast him an affectionate glance. Max had once lived in the real world where acquisition and money were king. Even though now he owned an inn he called the Place of Happiness, Max knew his inn wasn't the real world. "I'd like to think you still do understand my logic and my business. You used to be the number-two shark on Wall Street, right after me. Now you've become a bum, doing nothing all day but run this place. Why I wanted to come see you is beyond me."

Max burst out laughing. "You wouldn't have come to see me if you hadn't been able to combine the visit with the meetings. And by the way, just for your information, I always considered myself number one."

"In your dreams."

Max's grin faded. "Ginnie's a nice girl, Damien."

"You're not going to warn her against me, are you?"

"On the contrary, I feel like maybe you're the one who should be warned."

The setting sun tipped the waves amber and burned a touch of gold into Ginnie's reddish-brown hair as she leapt from the fishing boat into the thigh-high surf. "Thanks, Danny."

"Any time, Ginnie." The tanned, muscular man on the deck waved and headed his boat back out to sea.

She turned toward shore, then saw him, a dark figure on the glittering sand, dressed in a business suit.

Damien.

A shiver raced through her containing a warmth that defied the cold water lapping at her. He was standing with his long legs planted apart, his arms folded across his chest, and even from so great a distance, the piercing heat of his gaze penetrated her skin.

She started toward him, her heart pounding again. She accepted that *he* was the cause.

After the night before and what had happened between them, she had hoped to delay this meeting to give herself time to think. She had got up at dawn and sought out Danny, asking him if she could go fishing with him and his friends. But she had known Damien would find her, and in fact had eagerly anticipated this moment.

She was nearly on the beach when he walked into the water to meet her. A smile spread across her face. "Your shoes are getting wet."

"Really?" he asked, his voice low and raspy. "Who's Danny?"

"A friend. So is his wife."

"That's good." He couldn't take his eyes off her. He was considered a tough, sophisticated man, but nothing or no one had ever got to him as she had. The wet portion of her skirt clung to the curves of her hips and legs. She wasn't wearing a trace of makeup or lipstick, but her cream-colored skin with its peach undertone had a luminosity that was natural. And her eyes—

Excitement suffused Ginnie. There was no music now, and there was a sun instead of a moon, but there was still that deep, powerful pull of attraction she had felt for him all week and that last night had nearly spiraled out of control. "Your eyes are extraordinary."

He laughed. "They're plain old brown."

"They're *golden* brown."

He framed her face with his hands. "And yours are a lovely smoky green. The smoke hides dreams, doesn't it? I don't know why, but something makes me want to try and make your dreams come true." An electrically charged thrill coursed down her spine as she realized that, as extraordinary as it might sound, she was beginning to think he could be one of her dreams. But she couldn't tell him that. She gave a light laugh. "That's a great line you have there."

"I don't use lines."

Her throat tightened; there was no doubt in her mind he spoke the truth. "Apparently, you don't do things on impulse either."

"Why do you say that?"

"Each morning when I ran past you, I kept expecting you to come down and say something to me."

He slipped his hands into his pockets and tilted his head to one side. "What would you have done if I had?"

"Probably tried to run away from you."

"Then maybe it's a good thing I didn't, because you might have gotten away from me. I'm not in as good a shape as you are."

"I don't believe you."

He smiled with a tenderness that was foreign to him, but seemed exactly right in a smile for her. "You didn't run this morning, and I've been looking for you all day." In fact, he had gone half-crazy when he hadn't been able to find her, and he had finally decided to wait on the beach. It made sense to him that ultimately she would come to him here.

"I needed some time to breathe."

"Without me, you mean." The idea that she had felt the need to get away from him bothered him, but he could be patient when it was important. And she was definitely important. "It's been hours since I've tasted you."

He bent and pressed his lips to hers, and heat spread everywhere she had nerves. Their effect on each other was undeniable, she thought. How could she fight it? Did she really want to? They were two questions she had wrestled with all morning, but here it was afternoon and she still had no answers.

The waves spilled to the shore and foamed at their feet, and she forgot about answers as she wrapped her arms around his neck and opened her mouth beneath his just as she had last night, easily, willingly, gladly. If he needed her taste, she also needed his. She had never tasted anything like his flavor, yet in some way she knew it very well. It was the flavor of a mutual desire and an instinctive, unexplainable knowledge of the other. When his tongue plunged deep into her mouth, she twined her own around it, savoring the rough velvet feel, a mating in its own way.

When at last he pulled away, she stared at his lips for a moment, then looked up at him. "There was another reason I didn't run this morning. I needed time to clear my mind."

"And did you?"

She shook her head. "You're still there."

He groaned and pulled her back into his embrace, finding exquisite pleasure in the feel of the soft curves of her breasts and thighs against him and the fresh, sexy, female scent of her. The surf eddied around their legs and ankles, and it was long moments before he could bear to finally loosen his hold on her. But even then, he drew only far enough away so that he could see her face and smoky green eyes. "I was scheduled to return to New York today."

A gasp escaped her lips. "You're leaving?" Even though she had known he was only a guest at the inn, it hadn't occurred to her that he might be leaving anytime soon.

"Not now. I changed my plans." It had been hell to arrange, but he'd managed.

Her expression remained troubled. "When will you have to leave?"

"I can stay for a few more days."

"And then?"

He thought of his history of failed relationships; he thought of the life he had made for himself in which he had to answer to no one. Then he looked at her. "I don't even want to think beyond right now."

She nodded, oddly enough understanding and agreeing with him.

He chuckled with bemusement and shook his head. "I don't know what I'm doing. I've always been lousy at relationships. I don't know if I even want this."

An image of Nathan and Michael came into her mind, and with the image, their expectations. "I don't know if I do either."

Resolve replaced his bemusement. "I should have added that I don't seem to have a choice in this matter. And if by some remote chance, you feel the same way, then I guess we're going to have to work it out together. Do you?"

"I don't know. I think I do. . . ." She took his hand. "Let's go back to my place so we can dry your shoes and I can change."

It was an invitation, not the answer he had wanted, but he willingly accepted it. "I found a group of houseboats not far from here, but I didn't know which was yours, and no one was around to ask."

"Mine is the one at the end of the pier with the gardens."

They fell into step together as if they walked thus every day, but Ginnie felt her heart pound with a strange and entirely new excitement.

Two

The afternoon sun had dropped nearly to the horizon when they reached the small houseboat community in an inlet not too far from where they had been.

Ginnie's houseboat was a two-story redwood and shingled affair that was moored at the end of a long pier so that the back of it faced west toward the ocean. Barges overflowing with plants and flowers, were moored on either side of it. She had created an island for herself, Damien thought.

Inside the houseboat he found a large, light, airy room that had a natural, earthy ambience about it—like Ginnie, he realized. Textured linen and cotton fabrics had been used on the comfortable-looking sofas and chairs; arrangements of sea-shells were here and there; plants were arranged in every corner and hung from the ceiling. And every window offered a view of either the ocean or a garden and allowed sea breezes to bring scents of spices and flowers into the house.

"If I had imagined a place for you to live," he said, "I would have imagined this houseboat."

"Then you like it?"

He turned to her. "It's perfect."

Her throat tightened; her chest burned. His intensity was overpowering, yet she wasn't afraid. She had moved away from San Francisco and made a new life for herself. Then last night he had walked down the beach and into her life. He had liked her music. He had burned her with his kisses. And he looked perfect in her houseboat.

"How long have you lived here?"

"Two years."

His eyes glittered with dark lights. "Tell me there's never been another man in here before."

She swallowed, willing the muscles of her throat to relax. "There've been one or two." But none of them had ever charged the atmosphere the way he was doing.

"I hate that there've been men here before me," he said, a smoldering tension emanating from him.

"I said only one or two. And no one's ever been here more than once."

He smiled with satisfaction. "Well, prepare yourself, because I may never leave."

"I love the houseboat, but before this, I lived in San Francisco in an ordinary house, like everyone else."

His smile broadened, and in some ways she found the curve of his lips more overpowering than the tension he inspired in her.

"But you're not like everyone else, are you?"

For a moment she was stunned. He had put into words what she had always been made to feel. In the past similar words had always made her want to curl up inside herself and push the world away. But when he made the observation, she had felt a special warmth.

He reached out and touched her hair, then her cheek. "You're unique. A person would have to be blind, deaf, and dumb not to know that."

If he kissed her now, she thought, she would come apart. She searched for something else she could say, something that would bring normality to the air around them. "Take off your shoes and I'll put them on a rack in the dryer."

"They're leather, Ginnie."

"Don't worry, I won't shrink them. I'll set the dryer on air." A trace of laughter twinkled in the smoky depths of her eyes as she glanced at his shoes. "But anyone who would wear handmade Italian leather shoes into the water really deserves for them to be shrunk."

"Even if I did it because I couldn't bear to part from you a moment longer?"

She felt a wonderful kind of melting in her insides, and didn't fight against it. "You did the right thing," she said softly, then pulled herself up short.

He sat down, skinned off his shoes and socks, and handed them to her. She left the room to take care of them, and when she returned, she found him poking at a seashell mobile. She grinned at the incongruous sight he made, barefoot and dressed in a three-piece, impeccably tailored suit. "Did you come to the inn on business?"

He gave the seashell one final poke, then nodded, extremely reluctant to speak of any kind of reality with her. "I came to visit Max, but, yes, I am conducting business while I'm here."

"No one ever comes to the inn on business. It's more a place to get away from everything, to relax."

"That's what Max tells me, but I can conduct business anywhere."

"And do you always dress for it too?" With a gesture she indicated his dark blue pinstriped suit.

He tugged at a French cuff, insuring its proper position. "I enjoy suits."

"For beach wear?"

"Normally, the beach does not factor into my daily activities."

"Factor? Did you really just use the word *factor*?"

"Why are we talking about what I'm wearing?" he suddenly asked, his voice soft and husky.

She clasped her hands together. "I'll be honest with you. Things seem to be happening with us, and I keep thinking that these things can't be real."

"The kiss last night was real. The kiss a little while ago was real. In fact, Ginnie, if they'd been any more real, neither of us would still have our clothes on."

His directness stole her breath and heated her blood. "All the more reason to slow down."

A muscle flexed in his jaw. "Okay, I'll admit that I'm having a few problems with all this myself, and in principle I agree with you. But it's going to be hard. When I look at you, I feel like going Mach Three."

She glanced away from him, out the window, past the flowers to the sea, and thought of their kisses and the incredible sensations she had felt each time. Even now, there was an aching in her for him, and his gaze was positively scorching her. But . . . "I need to go the speed limit, at least for a little while longer."

"Then I'll try," he said slowly.

"Thank you."

He reached out and flicked a finger at a glistening strand of hair that curled and waved against her face. "To answer your question—"

"Which question?" she asked, surprised. She'd been so lost in thoughts of his kisses . . .

His lips twitched. "You asked if I always dressed in a suit."

"Oh, yes, yes I did."

"If you want us to slow down, Ginnie, you're going to have to help me out here."

"I'm sorry." She loved the way his lips took on an added sensuality when he smiled, she thought. And she loved the way his eyes looked when they twinkled. "Do you always wear suits?"

"Thank you. And the answer is yes. I'm as comfortable in a suit as I am in jeans."

"Do you have any jeans?" She couldn't envision him in anything casual.

"I must have. I have four closets in my New York apartment. There's got to be a pair of jeans in there somewhere."

"*Four* closets?"

"One for each season." He grinned wryly. "It's becoming increasingly clear that if I'm staying on here for a few days, I need to do a little shopping."

"I'll go with you." She had made the statement so easily, she thought, amazed, as if they were an established couple who did things together all the time—and even more amazingly, it felt as if they did.

"Good."

The gentle smile that played around his lips told her that he, too, was reflecting on the miracle they seemed to be. She felt intoxicated, shaken, confused, warm. . . . Almost as if she were falling in love.

"And we'll get you some shoes, too, since you don't appear to have any." His eyebrows arched in a playful way as he glanced pointedly at her bare feet.

"I have shoes, I just don't like to wear them."

"I'll buy you some anyway."

She shook her head firmly. "No, no, tomorrow is on me. You're a visitor in my town, and the least I can do is make sure you're properly clothed. We can't have you walking around town looking like some alien from outer space." She paused, her expression now serious. "You're not an alien, are you?"

"No, Ginnie," he said softly. "You won't get out of this that easily."

"Just asking." It would be a relief to find an explanation, however extraordinary, for the way they affected each other. She pulled her gaze from his and glanced vaguely around her. "Are you hungry?"

"Not really."

"I'm always hungry. I think I'll cook dinner. How does shrimp and fettucini, a tossed salad, French bread, and a bottle of Macon blanc sound?"

"Delicious," he murmured. "Just like you."

"Play for me," said Damien, his eyes on Ginnie. They were propped against a mountain of pillows as they sat on the floor, facing each other, their legs touching. Beside them, a fire crackled merrily in the stone-and-shell fireplace. The sound of the surf drifted through the open windows on a cool, gentle breeze and provided the only after-dinner music.

She shook her head, sending reddish-brown waves swishing over her shoulders. "I don't play for other people." She had changed into her favorite jeans that had been worn nearly white in places and a cream-colored silk blouse.

"You played for me last night."

"But I didn't know that I was." She slid her hand around the back of her neck and absently rubbed at the tight muscles there. "Look, it's no big deal. I just don't like to play for an audience."

"I've never heard anything more wasteful." He paused for a moment, taking in her set expression. Placing his hand on her leg, just above her knee, he felt her tension. Something was wrong. "You have a real gift, Ginnie. In fact, in case no one's ever told you, you're brilliant."

She worried her bottom lip with her teeth, thinking. Her music was a very private, intimate part of herself, and she had learned early that playing for others opened her up for exposure and put her in the position of risking disapproval. "I teach music," she said abruptly, instinctively steering the conversation in another direction.

"Really?"

She nodded, watching the way the fire created shadows on his hard, lean face, making him all the more fascinating to her. "I teach young people guitar and piano. It's a lot of fun and very rewarding."

"You must play for your students."

"If they need me to, I'll play whatever piece they are learning so they'll know what it's supposed to sound like." She glanced at the fire, her expression pensive.

Selfishly, he decided not to pursue the subject. It was as if there were a constant arc of lightning between them, but there was also a peace he had never known, and he didn't want to risk breaking it. He wanted *her.* The thought sent the blood pulsing hotly through his veins.

With great difficulty he cleared his throat and sought another subject. "You said you lived in San Francisco before you moved here. What did you do? Where did you live?"

"My mother died four years ago. My stepfather took her death very hard, so for two years after her death, I lived with him."

When he had asked the questions, he hadn't really cared what her answers would be; he had been simply trying to get his mind off of the constant need he felt for her. But in her answer he had heard a faint tinge of pain, and he smoothed his hand along her leg, comforting. "Were you and your mother close?"

She chuckled. "As close as opposites can be. My mother was a great beauty, perfect in everything she did, whether she was being a hostess, a wife, or a mother."

"No one's perfect, Ginnie."

"She was. Unfortunately for her, she had a daughter who wasn't. Poor thing, she was forever running after me with a comb and shoes and pretty hair ribbons."

She saw the frown that crossed his face and smiled. "It's all right. I survived. I was a gawky child. Now that I think about it, I guess I'm a gawky adult. I'm too skinny, and my arms and legs have always been too long. I'm forever bumping into things. And my mouth is too big for my face. And my bone structure is a little off." It didn't seem strange to tell him these things, though she couldn't remember ever confiding them to anyone else. "Now that I've told you practically everything bad about me, you'll probably leave."

He shot her a disbelieving look. "You're kidding, right?"

"No, actually, I'm not. As a child, I was forever hearing, 'Isn't she an unusual child?,' or 'She has such a different look,' or 'She's not at all like her mother.'"

He loved her music, and he realized he was hearing at least a partial explanation for the moodiness and complexity of it, but he still couldn't keep his anger from erupting. "That's the most absurd thing I've ever heard. How could they say things like that to you?"

"It wasn't exactly to me. The conversations were always meant to go above my head. Besides, they didn't mean any harm, not really."

"But they did harm, didn't they?" His growing feeling for her was giving him insight.

She exhaled a long breath. "I'm afraid I was very sensitive, and I've always had a great aversion to boxes."

"Boxes?"

"Boxes people try to put me in. Mother, bless her heart, sent me to ballet lessons and modeling lessons and deportment lessons. She so wanted a *polished* child. And my stepfather, Nathan, wanted me to be just like my mother. The pressure really increased after she died. He wanted me, and still does, to be the kind of woman who puts all her time and energies into being the ultimate homemaker and wife, as my mother was." She didn't add, he had her future husband all picked out for her—Michael, a man who would give her an ordinary, very pleasant life, with a house in the suburbs and an estate station wagon in the driveway. It was a life most women would give their eyeteeth for, but something had always made her fight against it. She shrugged. "I love Nathan dearly, but I had to move away from him to give myself room to breathe and time to find out what *I* want."

Damien leaned toward her. "You're absolutely the most beautiful woman I've ever known, Ginnie. As a matter of fact, I think you're perfect."

She threw her head back and laughed with sheer delight. "*You're* perfect for saying that."

"But it's true."

"Thank you. I almost believe you."

"Believe me."

Strangely enough, the softness and sincerity of his words soaked into her, soothing old wounds and calming new nerves. Who was he that he could affect her so? she wondered, studying him. "I've just told you some of my darkest secrets, but I don't know anything about you. Not really."

Deep inside, he supposed he was afraid that something was going to happen to spoil this peace and happiness he seemed to find with her. It was the reason he was reluctant to draw her into his world. But she had asked. He shrugged. "There's not that much to know. I live in New York City in an apartment I own."

She laughed. "And it's on the top floor of one of the tallest buildings in New York and it overlooks the whole world. Of course, it's the ultimate in elegance and design and, I'm sure, has been featured in *Architectural Digest*, and, oh yes, you have four closets, one for each season."

He chuckled. "See there, you do know me."

"Heck, that was easy. Tell me something about you I don't know."

"I buy and sell things for a living."

"And you're *very* successful."

He feigned annoyance, wrinkling his forehead with a frown. "Hey, you're too good at this."

"I'm sorry, but the four closets sort of give you away."

"Okay, how about this. I was born and raised in Brooklyn."

"You're kidding!"

He laughed at her astonishment. "I got you, didn't I? Well, it's true. My father's retired now, but he was a railroad conductor. My mother was and is a homemaker. They still live in Brooklyn, and to this day, they wonder where I came from."

"Why? Were you adopted?"

"Oh, no. I'm their natural son, but they've never understood where I get my drive and determination. I seem to have been born with genes that make me want to succeed. Most parents would be proud of a son who had accomplished all I have, but, though they've never come right out and said as much, mine are slightly appalled."

"Maybe what they don't understand is why you're *still* trying to succeed after all you've already done."

His mouth twisted wryly. "*They* don't understand, but you should. Just because you compose one song doesn't keep you from composing another, does it?"

"No . . ." she agreed hesitantly.

"There's always the next song for you, Ginnie. There's always the next business challenge for me. We're a lot alike. Our families may not understand us, but we can understand each other." His expression softened. "And when it comes right down to it, I'm beginning to think there's really only one thing I need. One *person.*"

Instantaneously, a flame ignited low in her stomach, and its heat left her breathless. "I'm not sure if I'm ready for all of this, Damien. For you and me. The suddenness of everything . . ."

He reached for her and pulled her around to him until she was cradled in his arms against him. He brushed her hair from her face, then allowed his fingers to linger in the silky depths. "Nothing like this has ever happened to me either. At this point I don't know if it's right or if it's wrong, and frankly I don't much care."

Just for a moment she was frightened. There had been a note of such determination in his voice, it had struck her as slightly ominous. And she had to wonder if he might possibly try to put her in a box of his own. Then he cupped his hand along her jawline and tilted her face up, and like magic, his touch allayed her fears.

He bent and pressed a warm kiss to her mouth. "Do you want me?"

There was definitely hard, unyielding granite beneath the softness of his voice, but his kiss . . . "Yes, but—"

He put a finger over her lips. "Sssh. No buts. There can't be anything more simple than our wanting each other."

With her cheek pressed against his chest, she could hear his strongly beating heart. Without having to be told, she knew he was a man with complete and utter confidence in himself, a man most men would be afraid to stand too close to for fear of being sucked into the whirlpool of his power. Given that, how could she explain to him the lifelong insecurities and doubts about herself that had been so much a part of her childhood and remained a part of her adulthood? She had made a life for herself here, but daily she battled her own vulnerabilities. She felt she had such a tenuous hold on herself, and she didn't want to lose that hold.

But then maybe, she thought, their seemingly

special connection to each other precluded an explanation.

He pulled her closer to him and kissed the top of her head. "I could never hurt you."

"Then, please, Damien, don't push me too fast."

Her vulnerability stopped him almost cold. He had never known anyone more special. She was worth the patience and whatever else he had to do to make her his, he reminded himself.

He bent his head and lightly kissed her lips. He would try to ease the pressure on her, he decided, but he couldn't release her.

"I've got a real problem." His smile hid the seriousness of what he was feeling. "Last night, despite all my intentions to the contrary, I went down to the beach to find you. Now I can't seem to leave you. Can I stay a little while longer?"

"Stay?"

"To talk."

"I'll make some coffee," she said with a smile.

The next few hours passed like a wondrous dream for Ginnie. They talked most of the night away, about nothing and about everything.

He made her laugh, he held her enthralled. But beneath the jokes and the light conversation, she could feel the strength and intensity of his desire, and astonishingly enough, she could feel an answering desire within her that matched his in every way. Before Damien, she had only released her passion through her music. But now . . .

The sky had lightened to a pinkish gray when she saw him out the door. And she knew that very soon she was going to have to make a decision about this man. And about passion.

• • •

"Hi, honey."

"Nathan?"

"Did I wake you?"

"No. Well, yes." Ginnie grimaced. The sound of her stepfather's voice on the other end of the telephone line was a definite intrusion into the dreams she had just been having, dreams about *Damien*.

"I'm sorry. You're usually such an early riser."

"I don't have any students scheduled for today, and I decided to give myself the morning off from running. But don't worry, I've got to get up in a few minutes anyway. I'm going shopping with a friend a little later." *What time was it, anyway?* She lifted up and squinted at the clock on her bedside table, but couldn't quite make out the numbers. She let her head fall back to the pillow. "How are you?"

"I'm fine. I thought I'd give you a jingle since you haven't called in a while. Michael says you haven't called him either."

As always, guilt stabbed through her when she thought of Michael. They had been childhood friends, and as they had grown older, their friendly love seemed destined to develop into something more intimate and lasting. Both families had expected them to marry. Nathan and Michael still did, though she had told them both she couldn't. But they were waiting patiently for her to get the urge for this "bohemian lifestyle" out of her system. "How is Michael?"

"He misses you. So do I."

She pushed up in bed and rubbed the back of her neck, trying to ease the familiar knotting pain. If she didn't love Nathan and Michael so much, she supposed their expectations wouldn't trouble her. "I'm only an hour's drive away."

He sighed heavily. "I know, I know. It's just that . . ."

Something in his tone managed to worm its way past her preoccupation with Damien. "Is something wrong, Nathan?"

"No, no, nothing I can't handle. Business matters, that's all. And I had to host yet another insufferable dinner party the other night without you. You know I'm not good at those things."

Expectations. Nathan had expected her to step into her mother's perfect shoes, run his house, and play hostess to his business associates. Michael expected her to marry him and do the same thing. "I'm sure everything was fine."

"The caterer wasn't very good."

"Use a different one next time." She saw the cream-colored blouse she had worn the night before hanging over the back of a nearby chair. She reached for it and brought it up to her face. As she had hoped, the silk held the faintest scent of Damien. The material had absorbed his smell as he held her against him last night, she thought.

"I suppose you've heard about the threatened revolution in Sagrado Montanas?"

"No, I haven't." She frowned, remembering the small South American country where Nathan's electronic company had a factory. She had visited Sagrado Montanas quite a few times with him, and had always loved it.

"Actually, the news organizations are playing it down, but we're getting daily communications from our people there. So far they say there are just a lot of rumors, plus a few skirmishes in outlying areas. And the government has given them assurances that they can keep the rebels under control." He paused. "Michael is chomping at the bit to go down and check things out, but I wouldn't feel good about him doing that."

She cast her eyes toward the ceiling, feeling another stab of guilt. Nathan viewed Michael as a son. "I wouldn't worry about it. There have been minor rebellions down there before, and nothing has ever come of them." She again lifted the blouse to her nose and caught a whiff of the exciting musk scent that belonged only to Damien.

"I'm really not too worried about it." He gave a small chuckle. "I don't have time to be. Someone's trying to take over my company again."

She groaned. "Oh, no."

"It's all right. I've fought attempts before and won, and I'll do it this time too."

"I just hate for you to have to work so hard, that's all."

"I might as well work. With your mother gone and you living away—"

"At the risk of repeating myself, you should really consider retiring, Nathan."

"What would I do?"

"Anything you wanted. It's the whole point of retiring."

"I don't think so. Not for quite a while. At any rate, I've talked enough about me. Tell me what you've been up to lately."

She pulled the blouse and thus Damien's scent around her, as if it would shield her from the guilt she felt at leaving Nathan alone. "Just the usual." He wouldn't understand about Damien. *She* didn't understand about Damien.

"When are you going to come and see me?"

"Soon, soon," she said absently.

"Is there any message you'd like me to pass along to Michael?"

"Tell him hi." It was the best she could do when the excitement churning in her stomach and her heart was for another man."

"I'm hungry," Ginnie announced as she pulled her car into a parking space and turned off the ignition. They were in the parking area of a group of shops that were built along the architectural lines of a Spanish mission and that formed a square around an old-fashioned bandstand and a small park. "You came earlier than I expected, and I didn't have a chance to eat breakfast."

"I'm sorry. I was kind of eager to get back to you."

Damien's wry grin added a dimension of irresistibility to his rugged face. Not that she had any thought at the moment of trying to resist him, Ginnie thought. "Kind of?" she asked, laughingly.

"I was most definitely eager to get back to you."

She smiled. "I'm not complaining. I'd merely like my breakfast."

"Then we'll get breakfast for you."

"Only me?"

"I don't eat breakfast." His gaze scanned the

stores. "I don't see a restaurant. Maybe we should drive a little farther until we find one."

"We can eat here. You're just not looking at the right places. And you need to eat breakfast too. Haven't you ever heard, it's the most important meal of the day?"

His eyes glinted with amusement. "Yes, I heard that—when I was in elementary school."

"Well, it's true."

"My mornings are usually pretty busy," he said almost apologetically.

"This morning's not. So we're both going to eat breakfast."

"Whatever you say. But I still don't see a restaurant."

"We don't need one. Follow me." She opened the car door, slid out, walked around to his side, and took his hand. "Our first stop is the bakery. Do you like pastries?"

"Uh, since I don't eat them, I'm not sure."

She laughed. "Then this will be an adventure. Let's go."

He couldn't think of a place he wouldn't go with her, he thought, falling into step beside her. Sandals adorned her feet, and her long, slim legs were showcased in the same faded, tight jeans she had worn the night before. And as if the way her jeans hugged her curves weren't enough to make his temperature rise, her top was a skimpy black lace affair that ended above the waistband of her jeans. To him, it seemed that she had been put together to form the very embodiment of feminine sensuality, and there wasn't a part of him that didn't respond to her.

In the bakery she chose an assortment of croissants, pastries, and a loaf of bread. At the produce stand outside the small grocer's, she chose two oranges. Next, she led him into a coffee shop where bins of beans and pots of fresh-brewed coffee gave off aromas that made his mouth water.

"What kind of coffee do you like?" she asked.

"Black."

She grinned. "You really are in a rut, aren't you? All I've got to say is that it's a good thing you decided to visit Max."

"That's exactly what I was thinking," he murmured, looking at her.

She laughed, then gazed at the different coffees. "We're just going to have to do some tasting."

"Hmm, as I said, exactly what I was thinking."

Something in his tone made her look up and see that his gaze was focused on her mouth. Her knees went weak. "Damien."

"I really do want to taste you."

"Coffee," she said determinedly. "We're going to taste coffee. And you'll like it too. For instance . . ." She poured him a small cup of Swiss Almond from a pot brewed for sampling purposes. "This tastes kind of like a candy bar, nutty and chocolaty."

He took a cautious sip. "It's good, but it doesn't taste nearly as good as you do."

A thrill shot through her, and she glanced around to make sure no one had heard him. "*Damien*, behave!"

"I thought I was. We're not on the floor with our clothes half off, are we?"

"No, no, we're not." She glanced vaguely around

the shop, wondering why that image appealed to her. "Would you like to try Amaretto?"

"No. The Swiss Almond was fine. Or why don't you choose one?"

The heat in his eyes was getting to her, making her crave things that had nothing to do with pastries and coffee. She needed fresh air, she decided. In the worst way. "Swiss Almond it is, then."

Minutes later, much to Ginnie's relief, they were sitting on a park bench, their feast spread between them, and plenty of fresh air around them. "There aren't a lot of things better than hot bread, fresh coffee, and an orange, are there?" she asked, popping an orange section into her mouth.

"I could think of a few things—"

Her lips twisted wryly. "Will you admit that this breakfast was a good idea?"

He grinned. "It was a good idea." When she looked as if she doubted his sincerity, he added, "Really. I can't remember the last time I ate an impromptu picnic. Maybe when I was in school."

"You learned you should eat breakfast in school, and you had picnics. It seems to me your school days were some of your best," she said teasingly.

But he took her seriously. "Not really. I was pretty serious, even then. Besides, my life isn't exactly chop suey now, you know."

She tossed a piece of bread to a sea gull and watched it lift into flight. "It sounds as if it's all business."

"To a point. But I love what I do, and that makes it entertainment. And now there's you. . . ."

Yes, she thought. And her, now there was Damien. . . .

Damien looked dazed. "Who would have thought there were so many kinds of tennis shoes?"

Ginnie picked a shoe at random from the display. "This one has metatarsal support."

"But how do I know if my metatarsal needs supporting?"

"I guess if you have to ask, it doesn't." She turned the shoe upside down and looked at the hefty price on the sole. With a raised eyebrow she replaced the shoe. "I knew there was some reason I liked to go barefoot. How about this pump-up version? It's supposed to hug your foot for better support. What do you think?"

Damien didn't even glance at the shoe in her hand. He was watching her and trying like hell to keep his desire for her under control. But just looking at her made his teeth ache. "I think I need to kiss you."

Her mind had been on the shoe display, and she looked at him in surprise, then threw a quick glance around the store. It wasn't terribly crowded, but still . . . "I thought we came here to shop."

"*You're* shopping, I'm watching you. You're not wearing a bra, are you? And you have an unself-conscious grace about you that makes me crazy."

Unused to such lavish compliments, she tried to hide the blush that came up under her skin by pointing in a businesslike way to the display. "I'm sorry, but there doesn't seem to be a wing tip in sight. *However,* we have high tops, we have low tops, we have in-between tops. We have leather, we have canvas, I think we even have a polyester blend here. We have black, we have white. We have shoes that will guarantee a slam dunk to make Julius Erving *and* Michael Jordan green with jealousy. And as I said before, we even have this handy-dandy pump-up variety. Do you want to try them? No, on second thought, I don't think I'd trust a shoe that hugged my foot. Well, let's see . . ."

Impatient to have the shopping trip over with so he could have her all to himself again, he sliced a hand toward a pair of ordinary-looking canvas tennis shoes. "Those."

She clapped her hands together with satisfaction. "Okay, good. Now we're making progress. Sit down and try them on, and then we'll go on to the jeans department."

"I don't want to try them on," he said firmly.

She gestured to a salesman, took Damien's hand, and led him over to a row of chairs. "You need to try them on, because more than likely you're going to wear a different size in these than in your handmade shoes."

The salesman was efficient, Damien found his correct size in two tries, and a short time later, Ginnie was pulling him toward the blue jeans section of the store.

"Just plain old ordinary jeans will do," Damien said adamantly, "and I don't want to try them on."

Ginnie nodded and gazed at the piles of jeans. "Okay, we have acid-washed jeans, we have stone-washed jeans, we have preshrunk jeans, we—"

"*Ginnie.*"

"Okay, okay. I think you need stone-washed,

preshrunk, if we can find them in your size. What is your size?"

"Uh, I'm not sure. My tailor—"

"Never mind, you can try several on. Now, we have a choice between straight leg, tapered leg, or boot cut. And as for the fit, we have relaxed fit, tight fit, sculpted bottom, molded thighs—"

"You're making that up."

"*Pleeaze*, how could you even think such a thing?" Enjoying herself immensely, she narrowed her eyes on him. "Turn around."

"What?"

"Turn around. I want to see what you look like from behind."

He grinned. "Ginnie—"

"Come on, come on. Men do this to women all the time."

He threw up his hands in defeat and turned around. "Well?"

She eyed his firm, muscular posterior with an appraising gaze. "Definitely tight fit, sculpted bottom."

He laughed. "Just give me the damn jeans."

She selected three pairs in graduating sizes and sent him off to the dressing rooms that were lined along the back of the store. After he'd gone, she threaded her way among the other shoppers, browsing until she had found several sport shirts and sweaters she liked, including a bulky gold cotton knit. At the curtain of his dressing room she said, "Damien, I've found some shirts and sweaters for you to try on—"

He reached out a hand and yanked her into the

dressing room with him, closing the curtain after her.

"Damien, what are you doing?" she asked with breathless laughter, then blinked. His shoes were off, and his slacks, shirt, and jacket were tossed over a large hook. And he was wearing only a pair of jeans, unzipped and hanging low on his hips, gaping open to reveal black briefs.

He took the garments from her hands and tossed them to a bench, then pushed her back against the mirror and pressed his body against her.

"I'm about to get that kiss I told you I needed," he said gruffly.

The contact was electric. He ground his lips against hers with a hunger that destroyed whatever defenses she might have been able to muster. She opened her mouth to his at once, because there was nothing else she could do. With him, her passion rose quickly, became urgent, and there was no holding back its tide.

Her sudden passion took him off guard. He had only meant to kiss her, but her unrestrained response had ignited a wildfire, and the flames were sweeping through him, destroying his control. "Lord, but I want you."

"Damien, we can't. Not here . . ."

"I know, but dammit, I've got to be able to have a taste of you at least. A *real* taste of you." He brought his knee up between her legs, lifting her as he balanced her on his knee, raising her top until it was bunched under her arms. Then he bent his head to her breast and drew her nipple into his mouth.

Her entire body jolted, and she stifled a moan as her head went back against the mirror. He sucked strongly at her, and at the same time, began to rock her against his leg.

Heat grew low in her body, and a tightening started in her belly. She quivered all over, unable to believe what was happening to her and *where* it was happening. She could no longer hear the murmur of the shoppers a curtain away from her. Blood was pounding in her ears. Breath rushed in and out of her lungs. It seemed so sudden, but in a remote part of her mind that still functioned, she wondered why this hadn't happened before. "Damien, stop—"

He raised his head. "Why?"

"Because we can't. Not here." She had said the same thing just seconds before. But now there was an urgent pleading in her voice, because she could feel herself weakening.

"Doesn't it feel good?"

"Yes—" Her voice broke.

"Honey, this isn't a fraction of what I can make you feel, and I want you to know it."

He kissed her again, long and deep and hard. The powerful muscles of his shoulders rolled and bunched beneath her hands as he moved her on him. Sharply sweet sensations stabbed through her, one after the other, each one jangling her nerves, building pressure, hurling her ever faster toward a place she'd never been before.

He broke off the kiss. "Tell me to stop and I will. Tell me, Ginnie."

She couldn't.

She pressed her mouth against his shoulder to stifle the sound of desire welling up inside her.

"Look at me," he whispered fiercely. He tangled his fingers in her hair and pulled her head back. "Look at me. I want you looking at me when it happens."

Her eyelids felt as if they weighed a ton, but she opened her eyes and stared into his and saw that all traces of the golden color in them was gone. Now his eyes were dark, pure black fire.

A moan escaped her. He captured it, keeping it for himself and letting no one else hear.

The swell of feelings within her was threatening to take her over completely. The heat and the tension were increasing and mounting. She had never in her life felt anything so . . .

"Is everything fitting all right?" The voice of the helpful salesman penetrated through the curtain.

With a sound of frustration she collapsed against Damien, every muscle in her body trembling, every nerve screaming.

"Yes." Damien's answer was curt and brusque as he rubbed her back beneath the lace top.

"Just let me know if you need a different size."

"Go away," Damien said with controlled anger. Then his voice gentled as he lifted her head from his shoulder and pushed the hair from her face. "Are you all right?"

Dazed and in pain, she felt as if she had just been in a terrible accident. A sob caught in her throat. "No, no, I'm not."

His expression went grim. "Let's get out of here."

Three

Somehow she managed to maintain her composure while she paid for their purchases and she drove them back to the houseboat. But she felt as if she were running a high fever. And Damien didn't seem in much better shape. His tension was palpable, filling the car, tangling itself up in her own agitation.

She was embarrassed, appalled, and stunned at what had just happened between them. Except in her music, she had never before let herself go to such an extent that she forgot everything but the feelings inside her. And the man who was making her feel them. Now she had almost let herself go, completely forgetting inhibitions and convention. . . . She needed to make some kind of decision regarding Damien, she reflected grimly. She rubbed the back of her neck. Maybe she was just kidding herself. Maybe there wasn't even the most remote possibility a decision *could* be made.

Forces of nature could not be transmuted to logical choices of the mind.

At the houseboat she set about with great purpose to stay busy. "Would you like something to drink?" She opened the refrigerator and peered in. "I have fruit juice, iced tea, wine—"

"We have to talk about this, Ginnie." He closed the door and took her arm.

With a cry she jerked away. Every nerve she possessed had risen to the surface, so that even a casual touch sent fire screaming over her skin.

"What's wrong? Did I hurt you?"

She flung up a hand. "No, of course not. It's just that when you touch me, I can't think."

"In our case, I've come to the conclusion that thinking is not necessary. Don't you understand that?"

"Are you hungry? I think I'm hungry again."

"I'm not hungry."

"I'll make chicken salad for us." Intent on getting the cutting board from the shelf behind him, she brushed past him, then had to stop until his effect on her senses subsided enough for her to go on. "I'm pretty sure I have all the—"

He took her by the waist, picked her up, and sat her on the counter cabinet so that she was at eye level with him. "I know what you're feeling, Ginnie."

She shook her head. "You can't."

His hands still gripping her waist, he positioned himself between her long, denim-encased legs. His expression was hard and determined, and his dark eyes were lit with fire. "Ordinary rules don't apply to us. I do know what you're feeling, because

I'm feeling the same thing. You want me and I want you. It happened that first morning I saw you running past the inn and you looked up and saw me."

"No, I—"

"You can't deny it."

No, she thought, she couldn't. So she kept quiet.

"I'll protect you. You won't have anything to fear or any reason to hold back. I want everything you have to give, and I won't accept anything less. For you and me, Ginnie, there should never be any holding back."

She couldn't argue with him anymore. She felt battered and bruised by the power and heat of the emotions that had deluged her this last week. Strangely, she knew he was both the cause and the healer.

All her life she had lived with a storm of feelings inside her. Her mother, Nathan, and even Michael, had never found her feelings acceptable, so she had suppressed them, letting them out only when she was alone and only through her music.

But now there was Damien. He had heard her play, heard all her yearnings, fears, passions, and he hadn't been repelled. He liked her the way she was. He wouldn't try to change her, to fit her into a box.

And he was asking her to let him share what for years she had kept bottled up inside. Leaving Michael, Nathan, and San Francisco to move here had required courage and backbone. But to give everything up to Damien would require even more. Could she do it?

"I've never understood love, Ginnie," he said

huskily, framing her face with his hands and gazing intently into her eyes, trying to convince her with the sheer force of his will. "The concept was slightly foreign to me. Loving someone more than yourself seemed impossible. Living and making love with only one woman your entire life seemed ridiculous. Then I saw you, and suddenly I knew what love was. It's *you*, Ginnie. Love is you. I love you."

"Damien—"

"Tell me yes."

Like a dam breaking, something gave way inside her. And in an instant everything was settled. "I'll do better than that." She maneuvered herself off the counter and past him, then turned to take his hand. "Come with me."

"Where?" For a moment he felt unsure.

"Does it matter?"

A smile slowly relaxed his troubled expression. "No. Actually, it doesn't matter at all."

She led him through the main room, then up the spiral staircase to her bedroom. Her brass bed was covered with a white down comforter, piled with eyelet and lace pillows of all shapes and sizes, and faced a wall of windows that looked out at the sea.

The surroundings registered only peripherally with Damien. Ginnie was his focus; she controlled his very heartbeat, she governed his very breathing.

She kicked off her sandals, unbuttoned and unzipped her jeans, then peeled the jeans down over her hips and her legs until she could step out of them. Her every move was a graceful seduction, he thought, made all the more potent because she was unaware of the true extent of her power over him.

Damien swallowed against a thickened throat. She was left wearing two things: black lace bikini panties that skimmed across the smooth, flat delta of her stomach and the black lace top that stopped just below her breasts. Then she raised her arms and lifted the top up and off. A surge of hunger tore through him that left him weak. Her breasts were high and firm, and he remembered what a perfect fit they made for his hands. His gaze touched on the tightened buds of her nipples. It hadn't been that long since he had had one of them in his mouth, drawing her into him, taking her taste as his very own. Like a junkie, he needed that taste again with a force that had him shaking and his control fraying. He could already feel himself pressing against the seam of his trousers.

But there was more. . . . As he watched, she hooked her thumbs in the top of her panties and shimmied the lacy scrap of a garment down her long legs and off, a pure female action that had his heart hammering. Then she stood naked before him, and his lungs burned as he tried to draw a breath. Her creamy skin was gilded by the sunlight that reflected off the ocean and streamed through the windows. Her hair fell in its usual disordered mass of waves, reaching almost to her breasts. Her legs seemed to go on forever, and the triangle of hair at their apex was the same color of glorious reddish brown as the waves that lay over her shoulders. Every muscle in his body was twisted with painful longing for her. Lord, he thought, if he didn't have her soon, he was going to explode.

She stood very straight and spoke softly. "Make love to me, Damien."

He tore at his clothes, discarding them as fast as he could. Every cell in his body was demanding that he bury himself inside her as quickly as possible. He swept her into his arms, placed her on the bed, and came down on top of her.

The comforter was soft beneath her. Above her, she saw him, muscled, hard, and magnificent, his face contorted with a savage expression. Unable to help herself, she tensed.

His eyes flickered with a fiery need, but his voice was gentle. "I know you're a virgin. I'll be as careful as I can."

Her eyes widened. "How do you know?"

"I don't know. I just do."

There it was again, she thought. The intangible link that could be neither explained nor brushed away. Nerve by nerve, she relaxed and spread her legs.

"I feel like I've wanted you all my life." His voice was little more than a rough whisper, and he touched her and found her already damp and swollen. "Are you ready for me?"

She slid her arms around his neck. "I think I've been ready for you all my life."

A rough, tortured sound came up from his chest. He bent and pressed a tender kiss to each breast, then lowered his hips and slowly began to enter her.

Her hands went to his back, feeling the powerful muscles that quivered with restraint beneath the sleek skin. "You don't have to be careful. I want you as much as you want me."

"That's impossible."

Her hands skimmed down his torso to his buttocks and clenched on him. "From this moment on, nothing will be impossible between us."

Sweat already gleamed on his skin. He had meant to be gentle, take her a little at a time so the pain he caused her would be minimized. But he couldn't. He simply couldn't.

He bent his head to her mouth for a deep, fierce kiss, and at the same time, drew back his hips and drove into her. She gave a soft cry, but he didn't pause. She felt like hot, tight velvet around him, and he began to thrust in and out of her.

The pain had been momentary for Ginnie, and the discomfort quickly faded, leaving an incredible shimmering pleasure that grew with his every penetration. In a way the feelings were frightening. They threatened to lift her up and spin her away—away from herself.

"Come on, Ginnie," he urged. "Don't hold back from me."

Her hips began to lift and fall in a primitive rhythm unknown to her before. But her frantic, undulating movements matched his with a perfection she didn't question.

A great swelling of passion held her body in its grip. Ecstasy rolled over her in continuous surges like great pounding waves that grew bigger and more powerful with every thrust Damien gave. Instinctively searching for an anchor in the storm, she reached behind her to grasp a brass railing.

"No," he muttered savagely, reaching for her hands. "Hold on to *me.*"

She wrapped her arms and legs around him and did just that, letting him become her anchor, even though he was also the storm. He rained kisses over her face; he murmured words she couldn't clearly hear, but she knew the meaning.

She pressed her fingertips into the muscles of his back, making impressions in his skin. His buttocks flexed as he plunged deeper into her; his body shuddered and clenched. He knew he couldn't stave off the inevitable much longer.

"Open your eyes, Ginnie. I want you looking at me."

As in the dressing room of the store, she obeyed him. How could she not? From him, she was learning the true meaning of passion, the true meaning of freedom.

Without letting up on the intensity or strength of his thrusts, he put his hand between them, touching her. Suddenly, she tensed, then arched up to him with a cry that tore through his brain and made him lose what was left of his sanity. She was incredibly tight around him, and when he felt her inner contractions begin, there was no holding him back. Like a madman, he drove into her, hard and fast until convulsions gripped him and he emptied himself into her.

The sun glided slowly, slowly downward in the afternoon western sky as if it were slipping through a vat of honey. From the bed Ginnie and Damien had a perfect view of the spectacular sight, but they were wrapped up in each other and caught only occasional glimpses.

Damien cradled her in the crook of his shoulder. "How old are you?"

She chuckled. "We seem to know so much that's important about each other, but we don't know little things like age. I'm twenty-six."

"And I was your first lover." His voice expressed amazement.

She threaded her fingers through the soft, springy hair that grew on his chest. "I don't really know why I've never made love to a man before. I certainly had opportunities." Thoughts of Michael flitted through her mind, how he had pressed her time and again for a physical relationship, actually a commitment of *any* kind.

"I'm glad I was the first," Damien murmured, and dropped a kiss on her silky head.

"I am too." And she was. She had never felt anything so right. "It was obviously meant to be."

She skimmed her hand down to the flat plane of his stomach, and had the satisfaction of feeling him quiver.

He captured her hand with his. "You're mine."

The savage possessiveness in his voice was vaguely disquieting, but the languor in her body made it impossible to protest. "How old are you?"

"Thirty-five."

"And there have been women . . . ?"

"There were, but I honestly can't remember them. Not their names or what they looked like. You're the only woman in my head and heart."

She turned her face and gazed up at him with a

smile. "I really, *really* like the way you answer questions."

"Is that all you like about me?"

"Oh, fishing for compliments, are we?"

"I thought maybe you liked the way I did certain things"—he smoothed his hand around her breast, then cupped it in his big hand—"like this, for instance."

"That is very nice," she admitted.

"Nice?" He said the word as if he had taken a bite of spoiled fish. He flexed his fingers in the softness of her breast, then brushed a thumb across her nipple and back again.

A shock of pleasure rushed through her. "Damien, what are you doing?"

"I'm only trying to find out what you like and don't like." He took the nipple between his thumb and finger and worried the sensitive nub.

"I like everything," she said breathlessly.

"But you must like some things better than you like other things. For instance—" He bent his head to her breast and drew the tortured nipple into his mouth, pulling, nibbling, sucking, filling himself up with her taste. When he was temporarily satisfied, he lifted his head. "How did you like that?"

"I loved it."

"Ah, now we're making progress." His hand went to her other breast and its nipple, treating the rigid tip to the same pleasuring as the other. "How much did you love it?"

"Damien—"

He pulled on her nipple. "Tell me."

Heat now encased her. All thinking processes had gone on automatic. "I *loved* it."

"That's good," he whispered, and maneuvered his lean, muscled body until he was over her, supporting himself on his elbows and gazing intently down at her. "But what I want, what I *truly* want more than anything else in the world, is for you to love my touch so much, to become so addicted to me and my lovemaking, that you can't live without it. I want to become so necessary to you that you can't breathe without me."

"That may have already happened," she whispered.

"*May* is not good enough." He lowered his head and pressed his mouth between her breasts, then trailed kisses down the center of her body, circling and dipping his tongue into the navel, continuing over her satinlike skin until he reached the enticing triangle of hair.

"Tell me you love me," he muttered, his mouth pressed against her.

The command reached her fevered brain, and she realized that if love was confusing, tempestuous emotions that made her feel as if she had been turned inside out and upside down, then she was certainly in love.

His mouth went lower. "Tell me."

"I love you," she whispered, knowing she did.

And then the world blanked out for her.

The afternoon and evening passed in a blur for Ginnie. They slept, they ate, they made love. Her body fairly vibrated with a glowing satisfaction. She'd never known such contentment, such complete happiness. "Let's go for a walk on the beach," she said suddenly around midnight.

"A walk on the beach?" Damien's long length was stretched out beside her in bed, completely relaxed. "Whatever for?"

"Fresh air."

"I don't want to go anywhere. I'm happy where I am." He pointed toward the French doors that led out onto a porch. "If you want fresh air, all we have to do is open them, although I think fresh air is highly overrated. Give me a good air-conditioning and heating system any day."

She came up on her elbow and gazed at him, perplexed. "But you were walking on the beach the other night."

"Because I was restless and in search of you. I've found you, and I'm not restless anymore."

"Neither am I. But I love the beach at night. It's such a *free* feeling. I love its solitude. I love feeling that its beauty is just for me."

The idea of her doing anything without him was enough to cause him to tense. "This time its beauty would be for *us.* I would be with you."

"Then you'll come with me?"

He sighed with the resigned knowledge that there was very little he could deny her. "If it's what you want, then yes, I'll come."

And by the rock where he had first seen her, he took her down to the sand and made love to her. To him, their lovemaking on the beach completed what should have happened two nights earlier. Now she was well and truly his, he thought, then wondered why he still wanted more.

• • •

Max draped his long body against a terrace railing and watched Damien come up the walk to the inn the next morning.

"Well, well, long time no see. Normally, if any of our guests had disappeared for twenty-four hours, I would have suspected foul play, but with you I decided that more than likely you were the one committing the foul play. Nice jeans, by the way."

"Thanks. Any messages?"

"A stack three feet high. Oh, and I've been just fine, thank you."

Damien climbed the short flight of stairs until he was by his friend's side. "I didn't spend a second worrying about you," he said, eyeing Max's tennis attire. "You have your life ordered precisely as you like."

"You're not doing too badly in that department either. All systems are still go on the takeover of Camden Electronics."

A twinkle sprang up in the depths of Damien's brown eyes. "You read my mail?"

Max flipped his tennis racket up in the air, caught it, and shrugged with studied nonchalance. "You weren't around, and I knew if there were any problems, you would want me to troubleshoot for you."

Damien burst out laughing. "And you were hoping you'd have to, weren't you? You may have retired from Wall Street, old friend, but ticker tape still runs through your veins."

With a grimace Max straightened away from the

railing. "I merely like to have a hand in now and then, that's all."

"Any chance of you coming back?"

"None," Max said flatly.

"What about if I have the powers-that-be put in a tennis court smack in the middle of Wall Street?"

"Throw in an ocean, and I'll think about it."

Damien gave a short laugh. "Yeah, sure, you will."

"By the way," Max said, "I saved the worst news for last. Your secretary says you're needed in New York pronto. Something about the Tokyo deal."

"*Dammit.* I can't leave yet."

"She sounded pretty frantic."

Damien's mouth firmed. "I'll take care of it."

An hour later Damien found Ginnie on one of her garden barges, watering her flowers. "Hi," she said, waving. "You're back sooner than I expected." She twisted the nozzle on the hose she held until the water stopped.

He crossed the little bridge that took him from the porch of her houseboat to the barge, then threaded his way among the flowers until he reached her. Barefoot, with her hair blowing in the sea breeze and her skin aglow from the sun, she looked more glorious than any of the flowers around her. He'd like to have her portrait painted as she was at this moment, he thought. "Something's come up, Ginnie. I have to return to New York."

She felt as if a giant fist had punched her in the stomach. The hose slipped from her nerveless fingers and fell to the deck of the barge. "No . . ."

He closed his long fingers around her upper arms, imprinting his possession on her as much as he was supporting her. "Don't worry. I'm not leaving without you. You're coming with me."

She should have seen it coming, she told herself; she was stupid not to have. It was as if she had been living inside a beautiful iridescent bubble, its dreamworld environment of their own making, and now an unseen force was trying to prick it. "I-I can't. My students . . . My houseboat . . ."

His hold tightened. "I *need* you, Ginnie. You've *got* to come back with me."

The ocean was calm today, but it seemed to her as if the barge had suddenly begun to pitch and roll. Her life here was important to her. Here, no one tried to mold her into being what he needed. Here, she had worked hard making her houseboat into a haven where she could be comfortable; it represented her independence. And she received immense satisfaction from teaching.

But now there was also Damien. She tried to envision what her life would be like if he left and she stayed, and she realized that nothing would ever be the same again. Her heart felt empty just thinking about it.

"Ginnie?"

She couldn't bear the thought of being apart from him, but to leave here . . . "It's such a big decision, Damien."

"I'm sorry I can't give you more time to think about it, but is it really such a big decision?" He plowed his fingers through his hair, the action revealing a small portion of his agitation. "It all seems so simple to me. One—I need to be back in New York by tomorrow. Two—I need to leave here this evening. Three—it's impossible for me to leave without you. One, two, three. Just like that. Easy, Ginnie."

She freed herself from his hold, and her hand went to the back of her neck, seeking and finding the expected knots. "This evening?"

"I'll help you. You don't even have to pack if you don't want to. Bring your guitar, and you can buy whatever else you need once we get there."

"The houseboat—"

"I'll get in touch with a realtor."

For a moment she was seized by panic. "I'm *not* selling. Why would you even think of such a thing?"

"It seemed the most sensible solution, but if you're not ready to sell, then we'll get someone to keep an eye on it. It's not important. None of these details are important."

"Maybe not to you—"

He grasped her arms again. "If it's something that's important to you, then it's something that's important to me. I'm only trying to show you how simple everything can be. For instance, my secretary can notify your students. Ginnie, everything will sort itself out, you'll see. Don't concern yourself with the mundane details. You weren't meant for the ordinary. I understand that, even if your family doesn't. I love you."

He had a way about him, she thought helplessly, a way of transferring to her his heat and passion so that it matched and blended with hers and became even stronger.

"Marry me, Ginnie, and we'll create a new life together."

"You're asking me to be your wife?" she asked, stunned.

His eyes blazed. "I don't think I'll rest until you are."

Four

It was as if she were standing in the sky, Ginnie thought. She reached out and flattened her palm against the curving glass wall of the master bedroom in Damien's apartment. The glass felt cool beneath her palm. Still. And, more important, real.

She had been in New York three days, and sometimes she had to pinch herself to convince her she wasn't dreaming.

The master bedroom was on the sixtieth floor of a concrete-and-steel building, cantilevered out over a large terrace on the fifty-ninth floor, which was also part of Damien's apartment. So was the fifty-eighth floor.

She slipped her hands into the pocket of her jeans and glanced around her. The bedroom was enclosed on three sides by greenhouse-type windows and offered a view of Manhattan that was breathtaking.

She gnawed at her bottom lip, feeling uncertain and apprehensive. Damien's apartment was as spectacular as she had imagined it would be, but she wished more than anything they could be back at her houseboat.

It wasn't as if she were awed by what she saw. She had grown up amid the trappings of wealth and power, though admittedly this was an extremely grand scale indeed. But she felt as if the world were spinning at twice its normal velocity, while she was still traveling at the same old speed.

Glancing at her watch, she saw that it was only one-thirty. "I wish Damien were here," she murmured.

The shrill ring of the phone interrupted her thoughts, and thankful for the diversion, she leapt to answer it. "Hello?"

"Hi, what are you doing?"

As always, the sound of Damien's voice made her heart skip a beat and drew a smile from her. "I'm alternating between climbing the walls and pulling my hair out."

"That bad, huh?"

"That bad."

"I"m sorry, I really am. I thought I'd be able to spend more time with you. Just give me a day or two more to wrap this up."

The guilt and worry that laced his voice made her rush to reassure him. "Don't apologize. I'll be fine. In fact, I think I'll go out this afternoon."

"No, Ginnie. Wait until I can be with you."

She rolled her eyes. They had been through this before. He didn't like her going out without him. "Damien, I'll be fine. I merely want to take a walk."

And *breathe*—which she found very difficult to do in his penthouse.

"Look, if you want to shop for clothes, I'll have several stores send over selections—"

"I don't want to shop. I want to get out and see something of the city."

"Then let me send my car for you."

"So I can do what?" she asked wryly. "Observe gridlock from the backseat of your limousine? No, thank you. I'll walk."

"I don't like this, Ginnie. What will you do if you get lost?"

"I'll hail a cab. Stop worrying, Damien. I've been to New York before."

"On visits with your mother and stepfather. This is different. You'll be on your own."

She could hear his tension increasing with each word he spoke, and she understood. He might as well have said, *You'll be without me*, because it was what he meant. He was obsessed with her, and she could almost trace the origin of his obsession back to that moment in the dressing room when their passion had exploded. Now he wanted to keep her in this ivory tower he lived in, breathing the air he had breathed, surrounded by his things, safe and untouched until he could get home and touch her himself.

She lived for the feel of his hands on her body and his mouth on hers. But there were times, and this was one of them, when she had the strange sensation of a box being closed around her, and she needed to get out of his apartment to exorcise the feeling.

"I'll be fine, Damien."

"I'll come right home, and we'll go together."

"You'll do nothing of the sort. You'll stay there and finish buying and selling or whatever it is you're doing."

"Ginnie—"

"I'm serious, Damien. You never know when you'll need another closet or two. So stay and make some more money, and I'll be here waiting for you when you get home tonight."

He chuckled. "Okay, but I'll be home early."

It had been a good afternoon, Ginnie thought, as she headed back to Damien's apartment around five o'clock. She had bought a hot dog at a stand and eaten it while chatting with a cabdriver, a banker, and two dancers who were with the American Ballet Theatre. She found some interesting shops that carried the odd and the unusual, and she had stopped to listen to a group of street musicians playing show tunes. Listening to them reminded her that she hadn't played her guitar since she'd been in New York. Even though Damien was at his office during the day, there was staff in his apartment. She missed the beach, her houseboat, and her students, she reflected, but most of all she missed her music.

A man brushed by her, hitting her shoulder as he charged ahead. Why, she wondered, did people in New York always seem to be in a hurry? On impulse she ducked into a bookstore, and ten minutes later had chosen five books and a couple of fashion magazines.

She was on her way to the checkout counter

when she made a stop to pick up a newspaper and saw a short article at the bottom of the front page stating that the situation in Sagrado Montanas was heating up. With a frown she added the newspaper to her armload. Then she caught sight of a business magazine and stopped cold. Damien was on the cover. Delighted, she scooped up two copies and made her purchases.

"I told you I'd get home early," Damien said as he strode into the bedroom later that evening.

Ginnie, barefoot, her long legs crossed, sat in the middle of the bed, surrounded by books and magazines, a stricken expression on her face.

He went still. "What's wrong?"

Wordlessly, she held up the magazine she'd been reading, the one with his picture on the cover.

His mind raced as he glanced at the magazine, then back at her. Genuinely perplexed as to what could have upset her, he shrugged out of his jacket and tossed it over a chair, then sat down on the end of the bed. "I don't understand what's wrong. Has something happened?"

"It's this article," she said. "They call you ruthless."

He stared at her for a moment, then burst out laughing. "*That's* what's bothering you? Ginnie, over the years people have called me a lot worse than that, and I'm sure they'll continue to do so."

"But do you deserve it?" She gestured with the magazine. "The article says you once took over a profitable company in Florida, divided it into pieces, and sold the pieces off. Hundreds of people lost their jobs."

"They were all qualified people. Within weeks I'm sure they found jobs as good or better."

"How do you know? Did you set up some sort of relocation program for them?"

He reached out, took the magazine from her, and flung it across the room. "Why are you letting something as silly as that damned magazine upset you? You should know how reporters can distort things. They pick a particular angle for their article, then slant the information in that direction. In this case, the reporter decided to make me look like a first-class bastard."

"He succeeded."

He shifted across the bed to her. "Ginnie, that article is biased against me. I refused to cooperate for it."

"They didn't interview you?"

"No. And even if they had, what happened in Florida is history, Ginnie. This is the present."

"But the article quoted more than one source as calling you cold-blooded in the way you conduct business."

"Practical men are always called cold-blooded."

"My stepfather runs a highly successful company, and he isn't the least bit cold-blooded—and to my knowledge no one has ever so much as leveled such a charge at him."

His brow furrowed. "Ginnie, I have to tell you I'm more than a little mystified about why you're so upset. *Why?*"

"I-I don't know."

"Nothing in that article has a thing to do with

us. A stranger wrote it. Strangers will read it. But it won't touch us."

"When you're with me, Damien, everything makes perfect sense. But when you're gone—"

"I can see I'm going to have to spend more time with you." He chuckled.

"Don't make fun of me."

He made a sound of distress. "I'm not making fun of you. Don't you understand? I feel the same way you do. I *hate* being apart from you, for even a few hours." He pushed a thick, shining mass of waves behind her shoulder. "Now listen to me, forget the article. And remember that no matter what I do in my business, I will never hurt you. I love you, Ginnie."

Her green eyes were even smokier than usual. "Sometimes I wonder . . ."

"What? What do you wonder?"

"I wonder if you really love me or if you're just obsessed with me."

With one hand he sent the books and magazines flying off the bed to the floor. Then he pushed her back onto the pillows and came down on top of her, supporting his weight with his elbows, and taking her face between his hands. "The answer to your question is, yes, Ginnie, I am obsessed with you, totally and completely. You're in my bloodstream. I don't think my heart can beat without you. But I also love you, more than I can possibly tell you. Don't ever doubt that."

As always, she found his intensity almost spellbinding. "I love you too."

The weight of his body pressed her into the mattress. His sensuality enveloped her. A heat began deep inside her, and unconsciously she moved against him.

He groaned. "Those jeans of yours are going to be the death of me."

She couldn't explain to herself exactly why she was in a penthouse high over New York City instead of in her little houseboat in California. And she couldn't explain exactly where this inborn need of hers came from to belong to him. With Damien, everything she did was pure instinct.

She moved against him again, this time knowingly. "Why? Don't you think I look good in them?"

"You look spectacular in them, but they're too damned hard to get off."

"I'll help," she whispered.

He started out to make their lovemaking tender, reassuring, but his needs ran away from his intentions. Somehow, between the two of them, they managed to get their clothes off and remembered to turn off the bedside light. But the room didn't fall into darkness. Millions of lights shone through the three walls of glass, illuminating their naked bodies.

And Damien made love to her all night long, trying in every way he could think of to put his stamp of possession on her. And still he wasn't satisfied.

In the morning when Ginnie awoke, Damien was gone. Determined to stave off the doubts that inevitably came when she was apart from him, she propped herself up in bed and saw a note lying on the pillow next to her. She opened it.

I'll be home early, and we'll go out and do whatever you want to do. I love you, Damien.

Looking out the windows, she saw a city that pulsed with energy. Last night, their lovemaking had surpassed anything that had gone before. He had vanquished whatever doubts she might have had. She had no idea how a man she had known for such a short time could have become so all-important to her. But he had. When they were together, they had the ability to shut out the world.

But she was alone now, and she needed to allow one small part of the real world in—Nathan.

She reached for the phone.

"Nathan Camden's office."

"Michael?" she asked, surprised. "Is that you?" An image of her old friend came to her—his handsome face with its strongly drawn, aristocratic features and his blue eyes that always conveyed such sincerity and openness. Then she realized she was talking to him as she lay in Damien's bed, naked, his scent still on her skin. She pulled the sheet up over her.

"Ginnie! I'm so glad I was here to pick up the phone. It's great to hear your voice. Nathan told me you had called and said you were going to New York for a few days."

She grimaced as she remembered the vague story she had given Nathan. "Actually, it'll probably be more like a few weeks." She had lost her sense of time. She didn't know or care what was going to happen tomorrow. She couldn't even think as far as a few weeks down the road.

"What exactly are you doing there?"

He sounded puzzled, and she couldn't blame him. "Nothing special. I just felt like a change of scenery."

"You gave Nathan the address and phone number where you're staying, but you didn't say which hotel it is."

"It's not a hotel. I'm staying with a friend." And lover. She should tell Michael about Damien, she thought, troubled about keeping the information from him.

"I didn't know you had a friend who lives in New York."

His tone was mildly accusing. She sighed. "Yes, yes, I do." She would rather talk to him face to face, she thought, but she didn't know when she'd be back in San Francisco. She had told him she couldn't marry him more than once, but he'd never believed her. Now, since Damien, it wasn't right to let him go on hoping. "Where's Nathan?"

"He's conducting a meeting in another part of the building. Ginnie, maybe you should consider cutting your trip short."

Expectations. There they were again. "I don't think I can do that. Michael, there's something I need to tell you—"

"First, there's something I need to tell you. Camden Electronics has been taken over."

"*What?*"

"The official announcement will be made soon, but it's a done deal."

"I don't understand. Nathan told me about the attempt, but he seemed confident that he could fight this."

"He tried. He drove himself night and day. We all

did, but I don't think we ever really had a chance."

"How's Nathan taking it?"

"On the surface he seems fine and is talking about looking forward to his long-overdue retirement. But I'm worried about him. Maybe you should come home."

Home. He was talking about San Francisco and the house on Nob Hill where she had grown up. But it wasn't her home anymore. Her gaze took in her surroundings. This penthouse in the sky didn't feel like home either. She felt like a displaced person with only Damien to hold on to. "I'll talk to Nathan and see what he says. But what about you? How are you doing?"

He chuckled. "I'm okay. The two hotshots who ramrodded the takeover say my position is secure, at least for a few months. No matter how much money or business acumen these guys have, they don't have my experience in Sagrado Montanas, and with the rebels rattling their sabers like they are, the new management can't afford to let me go. But I'm realistic. When my usefulness is up, I'll be history."

"You're highly qualified in *all* areas, not just Sagrado Montanas. They'd be fools to let you go, but if they do, you won't have any trouble at all getting something else, something better probably." Maybe Damien could help him, she thought, and made a note to speak to him about Michael.

"Thanks for the vote of confidence, but I liked it here. You know how much I think of Nathan."

The expectation had always been that after she and Michael married, Nathan would retire, leaving Michael head of the company. She gnawed at her lower lip, wondering if she should put off telling Michael that she had fallen in love with Damien. In light of what he had told her, she would be piling bad news on top of bad news.

"Ginnie, I'd really like you to come home. I need you. Nathan needs you."

But what about what I need? "Michael, I can't. Not right now, at any rate."

He was silent, then: "Is there someone else?" His amazed tone indicated the idea had only just occurred to him.

In truth she supposed there was no good time to tell him. And he had brought up the subject. . . . She drew a deep breath. "I didn't want to have to tell you this over the phone, but yes, there is."

"Who is he?"

"You don't know him. Michael, I'm sorry—."

"You can't be serious. You can't expect me to take this seriously. Dammit, Ginnie, come home."

"I can't, Michael. Maybe in a few weeks."

"No, now. If you won't come here, I'll come there. But, Ginnie, we have to talk."

"There's no need for you to fly here. Besides, Nathan needs you. I'm sure it won't be long before I'll be back, and then we'll talk. I promise."

"Ginnie—"

"Tell Nathan I called and that I'll call again soon. I've got to go now. Good-bye, Michael."

Miniature sailboats and yachts dotted the Central Park pond where Damien and Ginnie walked, hand in hand. A young man's jam box blared as he skated passed them. From across the pond a group of rappers were sounding out a song.

Damien lasered an annoyed look in the group's direction that would have stopped them cold if they had noticed him. "That's the worst racket I've ever heard in my life!"

Amused, Ginnie smiled up at him, taking in the compelling picture he made in the gold sweater and jeans they had bought just days before in California. "It's good music."

"Music? No, no, no. *You* play music. What *they're* doing is making racket."

"Don't be so narrow-minded, Damien. Rap is a legitimate form of music."

"Never mind about rap. When are you going to play for me again?" It was a question he asked her often. He couldn't stand it that she was holding a part of herself back from him.

"Would you be interested to know that rap is boogie-influenced?"

"No, I wouldn't, and quit changing the subject."

Her expression was all innocence. "I thought rap *was* the subject. Let's sit down for a while and watch the sailboats." She dropped onto a park bench and patted the seat next to her.

Damien sat beside her and put his arm around her shoulder. "I'm not giving up, Ginnie."

"I wish you would."

"And I wish I understood."

She supposed he thought her silly that she couldn't even articulate to him the problem, but keeping her music to herself was a habit of years.

"I've already heard you play, and I *loved* what I heard."

There was no doubting that his desire to hear her again was genuine, she thought, and his confidence in her went a long way toward bolstering her courage. But the memories of those torturous times when her mother and Nathan had made her play in front of guests were still very much with her. In her mind's eye she could clearly see the strained, sometimes appalled expressions on the faces of the guests, and she could remember how mortified and humiliated she had felt when she realized they had no idea what they were listening to. It hadn't taken her long to develop an aversion to playing in front of people, and soon Nathan and her mother stopped asking. Not even Michael had understood. Michael . . .

"You're a million miles away," Damien murmured.

She smiled ruefully. "Only about three thousand. I was thinking about an old friend, Michael Straton. I called my stepfather earlier today, and got Michael instead."

"Michael?" Just the sound of her speaking another man's name was enough to make him want to fight someone. "Who's Michael?"

"He's an old friend. We've known each other since we were children, and he's very dear to me. He asked me to come home, and I'm going to have to, soon."

"Why?"

"To try to make him understand why I can't marry him."

"*Marry* him?" He took her by the shoulders and turned her to him. "Why is there even any question about it?"

She shrugged, but his hands held her tight. "It's

all about the history of our two families and their expectations. Our marriage would make a lot of people very happy."

"It would destroy me."

She didn't believe him. No one as strong as Damien could ever be destroyed because someone he thought he loved married another. She paused in her thoughts, watching a small boy launch a sailboat with a push that almost landed him in the pond. *She wanted children someday*, she realized, and wondered if Damien did. It was something they should talk about. "I hated to tell Michael over the phone about us, but on the other hand, I didn't think it would be right to wait. He's waited long enough."

His pulse raced with apprehension. Losing Ginnie was his worst nightmare—*he*, a man who had never before had a single nightmare. His jaw tightened grimly. "But you've definitely told him you wouldn't marry him?"

"Yes, but I know Michael. He thinks he can change my mind."

The idea was so unacceptable to Damien, he barely heard it. "He can't, I won't allow it!"

"Damien—Oh, look, his sailboat is sinking. Where's his mother? Oh, shoot, she's over there buying popcorn. . . ." She jumped up and rushed to the boy's side, just in time to keep him from going into the water after his boat. She knelt down beside the boy, her heart turning over with sympathy as she saw the tears already welling in his big brown eyes. "You can't go in the water, honey. It's too deep for you."

His lower lip quivered as he pointed toward the center of the pond. "But I've got to get my boat."

"Honey—"

Damien thrust several folded bills at the boy. "Here. Go buy yourself another boat."

Tears began to spill down the little boy's cheeks as he looked at the money, then at Damien. "But I want *my* boat."

"Of course you do." She frowned at Damien, then quickly stripped off her tennis shoes and climbed into the pond.

Damien uttered an impatient oath. "Ginnie, get back here—"

She ignored him. "Stay right there," she admonished the little boy, "and I'll get your boat."

"Dammit!" Damien splashed into the thigh-high water after her. He caught up with her just as she reached the place where the boat had sunk.

She bent and scooped the boat from its resting place on the bottom. When she straightened, she bumped into Damien's hard body. "Good gracious, what are you doing out here?"

"Trying to keep you from getting hurt. Anything could be on the bottom of this pond. You could cut your foot or slip or drown—"

"Drown, Damien?" One brow arched skeptically, but her eyes twinkled with amusement. She emptied the water from the boat, set it sailing back toward the little boy, then gave Damien her full attention. "You're wet."

He was not amused. "If you didn't have this perverse attraction for water—"

Barely able to keep a grin from her face, she said, "Offhand, I'd say you were the one with the perverse attraction. After all, you're the one who keeps wading in after me." She skimmed her hand along the top of the pond, sending a spray of water over him. "Oh, look, you're getting wetter!"

The expression of surprise on his face broke her up, and her laughter turned to a shriek when he suddenly retaliated, slapping the water and splashing her twice as badly as she had him.

Barely able to talk because she was giggling so hard, she held up an admonishing finger. "Now, Damien, you don't really want to start a war with me. You'll lose."

A wide grin on his face, he folded his arms across his chest. "I guess you can dish it out, but you can't take it."

"Oh, yeah?" She started a wave of water toward him with a sweep of her arm.

The water hit him at hip level, and so quickly she didn't have time to plan a defense, he swept her high into his arms. "Say you'll marry me, or I'll drop you."

He had been proposing on a regular basis since they'd been in New York. But this time the mirthful lights in his eyes prevented her from taking him too seriously.

She feigned outrage. "I would never marry a man who would stoop to such underhanded tactics!"

He pretended to drop her, letting her bottom touch the water, before he stopped her fall and gathered her to him again in his strong arms. "Maybe you'd better rethink your position, or you could find yourself in the drink."

"I'll take the drink," she said, placing the back of

her hand to her forehead and giving her words dramatic emphasis.

Suddenly, Damien was stone-cold serious. "Marry me, Ginnie."

Her surroundings faded as all the laughter drained out of her. She knew exactly why she had told Michael she couldn't marry him. But she had no idea why she was so hesitant about accepting Damien's proposal. She loved him. He was everything she could ever possibly want. But . . . "Why do we need marriage? We have so much."

"We could have more."

She shook her head in disbelief. "Why do we have to do the ordinary?"

"Because until it's legal, I won't feel you're truly mine." There. He had finally verbalized, both to himself and to her, what had been bothering him.

She reached out and caressed his face. "But I'm yours now."

The simple gesture sent a shudder through him. "Then marry me."

"Do you want children?"

"What?"

"You see? We've never even discussed important things, like whether or not we want to have children."

"We are madly in love with each other, Ginnie. Using that love as a basis for our marriage, everything else will fall into place."

"Give me a little time, Damien. I can't explain it, but marriage to me seems the ultimate box."

"Ginnie—"

"Hey, you two, get out of there!"

She glanced over Damien's shoulder to see a

policeman waving at them. Grateful for the intrusion, she murmured, "Uh-oh. I think we're about to become jailbirds."

Damien exhaled a long breath and began wading back to the shore. "Try not to sound so happy about it."

Five

The next day after the maid had finished cleaning and had gone on to the floor below, Ginnie went into the bedroom, shut the doors, and reached for her guitar.

Barefoot and in her jeans, she sat cross-legged on the bed and began to play. And the music came spilling out of her.

Brilliant, shimmering chords expressed everything that was inside her. Layers peeled away to reveal layers. Her doubts and uncertainties wove through the song, adding emotional depth. Her passion added a richness and a complexity that was as powerful as ever, but more mature, more full-blown. And as she played, she realized the yearning that since the beginning had been so much a part of her music was almost gone. That indefinable something she had longed for had been fulfilled—by Damien.

Ginnie knew the moment he came in. He opened the door and slipped quietly into the room.

Her fingers faltered on the strings, then stilled.

She didn't look up. She kept her hands on the strings and forced herself to concentrate on the music that was still inside her. And to keep Damien fully in mind . . . for he was so much a part of what her music was now. He deserved to hear her play. And she *wanted* to play for him. Perspiration dewed her brow. She continued to try to concentrate. On the music. On Damien. And, gradually, she began to play again.

Damien leaned against the wall, feeling a quiet, deep joy and satisfaction. Listening to her, he was taken back to the night he had first heard and seen her play on the beach, and he experienced all the same emotions he'd had then. She touched places inside him that had never been touched before.

Her music filled the room and him. She was the answer to his restlessness, his emptiness, his longing. She was the love of his life.

She played on and on until at last the music was emptied out of her. She strummed the last chord and listened as the notes faded away. Then she looked over at him.

He pushed away from the wall, crossed the room, and came down on the bed beside her. "Thank you."

She smiled. "Thank *you*. You're the first person I've played in front of in years. It was a good feeling to have someone to share with. I'd almost forgotten how much I used to enjoy it before I realized . . ."

"I think I said it before, but I'll say it again.

You're brilliant. And you'll see. One day, you'll be able to play in Carnegie Hall if you want."

She laughed and shook her head. "I don't know where your confidence in me comes from, but you'll never know how much it means to me."

"You're very special, Ginnie, and I love you more than I can say."

Everything in her went soft, and her eyes misted over with tears of happiness. "Keep saying that often enough and maybe I'll believe it."

"Don't worry. I will." He paused. "I have a surprise for you."

Her expression lit up. "A surprise?"

"Yes. We're going on a picnic."

"A picnic? I *love* picnics."

He grinned. "*No.* Really?"

"Yes, really. But in Manhattan?"

"Well, not exactly Manhattan. More like Liberty Island. I've pulled a few strings, and it will be all ours when the park closes at four-thirty. We can watch the sun set while we eat."

"Damien, that's wonderful," she said, truly delighted. "How did you ever come up with such a marvelous idea?"

"I tried to think of something that wouldn't be ordinary, something that you'd like."

"You're incredible," she said softly.

"And you're beautiful."

"You almost make me believe it."

The next night Ginnie gazed curiously at the big white box Damien had laid on the bed. "What is it?"

YOU GET SIX
ROMANCES RISK FREE...
Plus AN EXCLUSIVE TITLE FREE!

Loveswept Romances

AFFIX
RISK FREE
BOOKS
STAMP
HERE.

Kay Hooper's
**Larger
Than
Life**

This FREE gift
is yours to keep.

MY "NO RISK" GUARANTEE

There's no obligation to buy and the free gift is mine to keep. I may preview each subsequent shipment for 15 days. If I don't want it, I simply return the books within 15 days and owe nothing. If I keep them, I will pay just $2.25 per book. I save $3.00 off the retail price for the 6 books (plus postage and handling, and sales tax in NY).

**YES! Please send my six Loveswept novels
RISK FREE along with my FREE GIFT
described inside the heart!** **RA12**   41228

NAME_____

ADDRESS_____ APT_____

CITY_____

STATE_____ ZIP_____

"It's another surprise. Open it." He watched her closely, anxious about her reaction.

She lifted the lid and let out a gasp of admiration. An emerald-green strapless evening gown lay shimmering within the folds of the tissue paper. "It's lovely, Damien!"

His smile held relief. He'd never actually purchased a present for a woman. Before this, his secretary had always done his gift shopping for him. But for Ginnie, he'd wanted to do the shopping himself. "I was hoping you'd like it."

"I do, but . . . why?"

"You bought me clothes in California. I decided I wanted to buy you something here. Besides, I'd like you to wear it for me tonight. Will you?"

"Where are we going?"

"Nowhere. We're going to stay home. You don't even have to wear shoes if you don't want to, but I would love to see you in the gown."

She glanced at him, then back at the gown, her excitement rising. Since she'd been in New York, she had been practically living in her jeans. She loved her jeans, but she didn't know a single woman who wouldn't jump at the chance to wear such a breathtaking gown. "What's the occasion?"

"Actually, it's a very grand event, but as I told you, it's a surprise. I will let you in on this much, though. The surprise is going to happen up on the roof garden."

Her eyes narrowed with playful assessment. "What are you planning now?"

"I guess you'll just have to come with me and find out, won't you?"

• • •

The silk of her gown rustled around Ginnie as she stepped through the door Damien held and out onto the roof garden. Oriental carpets lay over huge square quarry tiles. Everywhere she looked, candles burned, and tiny white fairy lights twinkled in the boughs of trees, planted in huge paneled planters. Roses and hydrangea climbed trellises. Baskets spilled over with ferns and geraniums. Large pots of shrubbery dotted the wrought-iron railing, and beyond lay the New York City skyline.

"It's like being in an enchanted garden on top of the world," she said, awed and utterly delighted.

"I was hoping you'd like it," he murmured, taking her hand and pressing a kiss to the palm.

"I do. You said a grand event?"

He held her hand tightly, reassuringly. "I consider it a grand event. A concert. I was hoping you would play for me."

Habits died hard. Her hand flew to the back of her neck and the growing knots. "Play . . . for you?"

He replaced her hand with his on her neck and rubbed soothingly. "You don't have to, but I was hoping . . ."

He led her toward the center of the roof where there was an exquisite silk Persian carpet; it felt like a cloud beneath her bare feet. Her guitar was propped against a red velvet wing-backed chair.

She gnawed her bottom lip. "I don't know, Damien. I played for you yesterday, but I had already started when you came in."

Tenderly, he cupped a hand along her jawline. "Nothing's different. It's just me and you here. And you know me better than anyone on earth, and you know you have nothing to fear from me. No one loves you more than I do." He eased her into the chair, then dropped down on the carpet at her feet. "Play for me, Ginnie."

She stared at him for a long minute, thinking what an extraordinary man he was. The candles, fairy lights, and flowers seemed at odds with the tough, hard man she knew him to be. But then, besides passion, he had shown her only gentleness.

She lifted her guitar and nestled it against her. She picked at a string, then stopped. After a moment she picked at another, then glanced at Damien. His expression was pure encouragement and love. Slowly, softly, she began to play. A spring breeze blew across the roof garden that rustled the silk of her skirt and tossed the waves of her hair.

And, gradually, in the breeze, a melody took form, its essence the happiness she felt, its power the love she felt for Damien. The chords rang strong and true out into the night. She played with a depth and breadth that she had never before had, creatively shading emotion into the music so that it resounded with elegance and a rare, moving beauty.

Damien was enthralled. He absorbed her music as if it were a life-giving substance, and he drank in the sight of her as if he could imprint the image of the moment on his brain forever. He had never seen her more radiant, with lights all around her and even brighter lights within. He wanted her so badly, he found himself shaking. He needed her so badly, he found himself afraid. If she should ever leave him. . . .

The song ebbed to its end. Ginnie played the last chord, then after a moment raised her head.

And the realization hit her: She hadn't just been playing for Damien.

Her music had carried beyond the roof to all the other roofs and windows and lights of the city and the people behind them. In a way, she had just played for all of New York City. And all because of Damien.

She looked down at him and realized he had known exactly what he had done, and her heart welled with love. "No one has ever understood me as you do. You've given me an incredible gift tonight."

His expression was solemn and intense. "I have another gift for you." He pulled a black velvet box from his pocket and flicked it open to reveal an emerald-cut diamond ring, its sparkle as bright and dazzling as any of the lights around her. "Marry me, Ginnie. Say you'll be my wife."

She set the guitar aside and went down to him and into his arms. "Yes," she said.

And in the warm spring night, on the silk and velvet carpet in the sky, they made love.

Ginnie hurried down the circular marble stairway and into the spacious living room. Rushing over to the tall, well-dressed man waiting for her, she said, "Michael, I couldn't believe it when the maid said you were here."

He stood rigid and unsmiling in the center of the room, his cold tone conveying a controlled anger. "I told you I would come here. I thought we needed to talk."

She made a vague gesture with her hand, a reaction to the ache of regret in her that she had hurt him. "Michael, I'm sorry, but I said everything I had to say over the phone."

His eyes had followed her hand and the diamond that sparkled there. "Apparently not everything. For instance, you didn't tell me the *friend* you were staying with was Damien Averone."

Her brow furrowed, because his anger at her and their situation didn't seem to fully explain the way his tone changed to intense dislike when he said Damien's name. "Have you met him?"

"Not personally, but his reputation and the actions that back up that reputation are enough to convince me I don't want to know him. And quite frankly, Ginnie, he's the last person in the world I would have expected you to take up with. He's scum."

Anger flared in her. "I know you're upset, but you said yourself you don't know Damien. He's a wonderful man, and I'm going to marry him."

Michael's gaze cut to the huge diamond on her hand, then back to her. "You've got to be out of your mind. How could you be sleeping with a man who—"

Abruptly, she flung up a hand. "Let's get one thing perfectly straight. Who I do or do not sleep with has nothing to do with either you or Nathan."

"Good Lord, Ginnie, what's *happened* to you? You used to care about the people who love you."

"I still do. Nothing will ever change that. But I have a right to live my life the way I want."

He eyed her sadly. "If that's the way you feel about it, then I guess there's nothing more I can say. But you realize, don't you, that there's no way Nathan will ever give you his blessing."

"I sincerely hope you're wrong about that."

Michael made a sound of disbelief. "What kind of dreamworld are you living in, Ginnie? Averone is a shark who chews people up and leaves only bones behind. Nathan and I know that firsthand, and you should damned well know it too."

"Oh, Lord, Michael"—disgust permeated her tone—"I saw the magazine article, but none of it's true. They didn't even interview him."

"What in the hell are you talking about?"

"Damien. The man I love. The man I'm going to marry." She put her hand on his arm. "I know I've hurt you, and I wish to heaven there'd been another way. But we've known each other since we were kids. If anything were going to happen between us, it would have happened by now. I take full blame because my insecurities kept me from expressing myself more firmly with you. But remember, Michael, I moved away two years ago. Maybe, just maybe, it's been you who's been living in a dreamworld."

Damien stood in the foyer, his gaze riveted on Ginnie and the man. He couldn't hear what they were saying. In fact, he could barely get his mind past the sight of Ginnie standing close to another man, her hand on his arm, talking intimately with him. Then he saw her stand on her tiptoes and kiss him, and a red haze lowered around him.

"I'm sorry, Michael," Ginnie whispered. "You're very special to me and always will be. Try not to hate me."

Michael covered her hand with his. "I could never do that."

"Ginnie?"

Damien's quiet voice brought her head around. "Damien, I didn't know you were home."

With the knowledge that Michael's hand still covered hers, it took a great deal of effort to force a pleasant smile to his face. "And I didn't know we were expecting a guest."

It was natural for Ginnie to tuck her hand in Michael's arm as she turned to face Damien. "Michael's visit was unexpected, but I'm glad you're both here so I can introduce you. Damien, this is a very dear friend of mine, Michael Straton. Michael, this is Damien Averone." Ginnie looked from one man to the other, and for a moment she didn't think they were going to shake hands.

At last Damien extended his hand. "Straton."

After a brief but obvious hesitation, Michael took his hand. "I suppose it was inevitable that we meet."

Ginnie rushed to try to relieve the open hostility between them. "Michael, how long do you plan to be in town? Maybe we could—"

"I have to leave right away," he said, his gaze still on Damien. "Nathan's going to need me."

"I'll call him. I've been meaning to—"

"No," he said, finally looking at her. "I think I'd

better break this news to him. It needs to be done in person and gently. Wait a few days, then call him." He bent his head and pressed a light kiss to her lips. "Call me if you need me."

Ginnie's eyes misted over as she watched Michael leave. He was such a good man, she thought. She hoped and prayed he found someone he could love as much as she loved Damien.

"You're crying," said Damien, barely able to keep his fury under control. *They had kissed each other twice.* "Why?"

"I care for him a great deal. I didn't like hurting him."

Very methodically, he brushed his thumb beneath her eyes, gathering up every drop of moisture he could. Then he lowered his head for a kiss meant to wipe all traces of the other man's kiss away. He ground his lips against hers, plunging his tongue into the moist open cavern of her mouth, reestablishing his territory in a totally male, purely primitive way. And only when he was confident he had succeeded did he raise his head. "We're going to be married tonight," he said.

"But we only had our blood tests two days ago." His kiss had brought her pulses to a racing point, and she could barely think.

"I've pulled a few strings and had the paperwork expedited. Everything's arranged." He devoured her lips with his gaze, a moment away from claiming them again.

"But I haven't chosen a dress yet, and I really wanted to give Nathan a chance to get used to the idea so that he could be here."

His head snapped up. "Straton didn't seem to think your stepfather would take well to the idea of our getting married, and I don't want to wait until he does. My parents are out of the country at the moment. So neither of us will have family at the ceremony. As for your dress, I've chosen one for you."

"When have you had time to go shopping?" she asked, astounded.

"I bought it at the same time I bought your green evening gown. I hope you don't mind."

"I'm sure I'll love it," she said, feeling dazed and breathless. But then, she reflected wryly, she had been feeling that way ever since she had met him. "Should I ask where the ceremony is taking place, or should I just let that be a surprise too?"

He groaned. "I'm sorry, Ginnie. I'm so eager to be married to you, I completely forgot that brides like to plan their weddings."

Her lips curved into a knowing smile. "You didn't forget, Damien."

He slowly smiled. "No, you're right, I didn't. But like I told you, I can't seem to rest until I make you my wife."

She thought only for a moment. "Then it looks like you'll be able to rest tonight."

"You'll marry me? You're not upset?"

"Yes. No. Are you going to tell me where we're getting married?"

"I thought the roof garden would be nice. I have people working up there now." He paused. "You won't have to wear shoes if you don't want to."

She laughed. "For my wedding, I'll wear shoes."

• • •

An hour later, Damien, alone in his study, picked up the phone and placed a call to his executives in his newly acquired company, Camden Electronics, and gave a terse order.

That evening Ginnie donned the ivory, jewel-encrusted satin-and-chiffon bridal gown that Damien had chosen for her. It settled around her, a glittering and gleaming confection, a symbol of all her dreams.

On the roof diaphanous walls of silk and tall panels of flowers had been erected around the cloudlike carpet, providing them with an exotic wedding chamber with heaven as their roof.

Ginnie had met the minister only briefly before the ceremony, but she believed with all her heart in the words he asked her to speak.

". . . love, honor, and cherish . . . till death do us part."

The lights of the city had begun to fade, and the new day was beginning to appear through the glass walls of the bedroom. Damien pressed his mouth against Ginnie's ear and whispered, "Where do you want to go on our honeymoon?"

Languorously, she lifted her arms and stretched, her naked body gleaming like a fine piece of polished ivory. "Actually, I've grown very fond of this bed."

He chuckled. "I'm serious. My jet can take us anywhere in the world. Name a place."

She turned her head along the pillow and fixed dreamy green eyes on him. "Damien, we've spent all night making love. It's hard for me to contemplate walking across the room, much less flying around the world."

He raised himself up on an elbow and curled a reddish-brown strand of her hair around his finger. "I'm not talking about in the next hour."

"That's good. That's very good."

He tugged playfully on the strand. "Just pick a route, or a country, or an area of the world, and I'll make arrangements. Two days tops, and I'll have everything taken care of."

"I didn't know you liked to travel so much."

"It's not about traveling. It's about having a honeymoon."

"Am I missing something here? It seems to me that if we're going somewhere that requires a jet to take us, we would, in fact, be traveling."

He released her hair and lifted her left hand where the heavy diamond-and-gold band rested along with the emerald-cut diamond. "We were married last night. We said our vows in front of a minister and God. The next step is the honeymoon."

"Step?"

He dropped her hand, grasped her chin, and gazed deeply into her eyes. "With you and our marriage, I want to do everything right. Nothing is more important to me." His grip tightened. "I'm going to make you so happy, you'll never leave me."

She pulled his hand away and threaded her fingers through his. "Why would I leave you?"

"I don't know, and I don't want to find out either." He had thought he would feel more secure about her after the wedding, that marrying her would provide him with the complete confidence to believe she would be his forever. And to a great extent he did feel satisfied. But vague shadows of doubts remained, to surface at odd moments. "So where would you like to go? What would you like to see?"

She sighed good-humoredly and pointed upward. "You mean besides this ceiling?"

"Ginnie, have you ever considered the possibility that there are a lot of other ceilings in the world?"

She smiled. "No, but now that you've brought it up, it does sound like a good idea. We could do a study of the world's most interesting ceilings."

With a grin he pulled her into his arms. "Trust me, you'll get to see *plenty* of ceilings."

The ringing of the phone woke Ginnie up from a nap. She glanced around the room for Damien, then heard the water running in the shower. She reached for the phone. "Hello?"

"Ginnie, it's Marcus Shelby."

"Marcus," Ginnie said, surprised, "how nice to hear from you." Marcus was a longtime friend of Nathan's and executive of Camden Electronics and she had known him for years, but she couldn't imagine why he would be calling her.

He cleared his throat. "I'm afraid I have some

bad news for you, honey. It's Nathan. He had a heart attack two hours ago."

"Oh, no!" She sat straight up in bed. "How is he? He's going to be all right, isn't he?"

"I hope so. It's a little early to tell yet what sort of damage has been done, but he's in intensive care, and the hospital has an excellent reputation. I wasn't sure if I should call you or not. Given the circumstances, I've had the impression that you and Nathan were estranged. . . ."

"Estranged? Good heavens, *no*." Her brow wrinkled, wondering where he had gotten such an odd idea.

"Good, then I'm glad I called." He hesitated. "I understand you're newly married, but do you think you'll be coming back here to see Nathan?"

"What are you thinking about, Marcus? Of *course* I'm coming. I'll be there in a few hours. I'll see you then." She slammed down the phone and swung her legs over the side of the bed.

Damien walked into the room, a towel wrapped around his waist, another towel around his shoulders, a frown on his face. "You'll see who when?"

"My stepfather has had a heart attack and is in intensive care. I've got to fly to San Francisco immediately." A list of things she had to do scrolled at top speed through her mind. Take a bath, pack, dress. . . . She started to get up, but sat back down and reached for the phone. "I need to make reservations."

He gently took the phone out of her hand and hung it up. "You're my wife now. My jet is at your disposal."

She stood and slipped her arms around his

waist. "Thank you. I'm so upset, I guess I'm not thinking too clearly." She pulled back a little and looked up at him. "I'm sorry I have to leave right now. I know you wanted to go on a honeymoon."

"We'll have our honeymoon as soon as you find out your stepfather is going to be all right. And you're not leaving me. I'm going with you."

Six

Ginnie gazed through the intensive-care window at Nathan and almost sobbed aloud. A dense thicket of tubes and cords connected her stepfather to an array of frightening-looking machines.

"The takeover was too much for him," said Marcus at her side. "And then your announcement of your hasty marriage . . ."

"Where's Michael?"

"When he got back from New York, he spoke with Nathan, then left again almost immediately to go out of the country on business. But we've cabled him."

"Good. He'll want to be here."

"And by the way, where is your new husband?"

The heavy censure she heard in Marcus's voice made her turn from the window and look at him. He was a man in his early sixties, as Nathan was, but with a thicker waistline and more gray in his hair. He had always been like a kindly uncle to her.

"I asked him to wait for me in the main waiting room downstairs." She had remembered the tension when Damien and Michael had met, and hadn't wanted a repeat of the situation.

Marcus nodded with approval. "I'm glad. I don't think it would be a good idea for Nathan to see Averone until he's out of the woods and feeling stronger."

She shook her head in denial of what he was saying. "I knew Nathan would be disappointed because I didn't marry Michael, but you can't make me believe that Nathan's heart attack was in any way brought on because I didn't."

"It was an accumulation of things, Ginnie, plus *who* you married."

She stared at Marcus, perplexed. "Who I married?"

"Mrs. Averone?"

Ginnie threw a blank glance at the nurse who had come up beside her, and it took a moment before she responded to her brand-new name. "Yes?"

"Your stepfather is awake now and you can see him, but only for a few minutes."

"Thank you."

Marcus patted her on the arm. "Try not to say anything to upset him."

It had to be the shock of Nathan's heart attack, she thought, but Marcus seemed to be saying the strangest things. "I won't."

She entered the room and walked quickly toward the bed. She had been nine years old when her mother and Nathan had married. He had been a handsome, strong, vital man then, and her image of him had never changed, despite the passage of seventeen years. But now he seemed a ghost of the man she remembered, pale and terribly frail.

Careful not to disturb any of the life-sustaining apparatus connected to him, she bent over the bed and took his hand. "Nathan, it's Ginnie."

His eyelids fluttered, and his lips moved as if he wanted to speak.

"I just can't turn my back on you for a minute, can I?" she teased gently, attempting to hide her distress. "If you wanted to see me this badly, you should have called."

"I tried."

His voice was weak and his words were slurred, but she could understand him. She gently smoothed her hand across his brow. "You did? When?"

"When Michael . . . told me . . ."

Told him about her marriage, she thought, wondering why she hadn't received the call. "We'll talk about it in a few days, but for now I want you to concentrate on getting better. Okay?" His eyes slowly closed. Tears gathered in her eyes at the evidence of how weak he was, but she hurriedly brushed them away. "I'm going to go for now so that you can get some rest, Nathan, but I'll be back. I simply wanted you to know that I'm here and I'll be staying until you're better."

She was pulling back from the bed when he surprised her by opening his eyes again. "It's ironic . . ." He stopped to moisten his lips, then started again. "The two things I care about . . . most . . . have ended up in the same . . . hands . . . I couldn't save either of you." His eyelids shut.

Ginnie stared at him, her brow pleated with consternation, and a cold dread beginning to seep through her. But when he didn't say anything else, she quietly left.

Marcus was waiting for her. "How did it go?"

"He spoke with me, then fell back asleep." She paused. "Marcus, he said the oddest thing. He said that his company and I had fallen into the same hands."

He nodded. "I told you, it was too much for him."

The cold was increasing; she wrapped her arms around herself. "Just *whose* hands are we talking about here, Marcus?"

He looked at her in surprise. "Why Damien Averone's, of course."

"*Damien* took over Camden Electronics?"

Marcus blinked. "How could you not know?"

An intelligent question, Ginnie thought. Too bad she didn't have an intelligent answer for him.

She couldn't remember taking the steps necessary to get her from the intensive-care unit to the first floor, but she must have, because when she reached the waiting room, she found Damien on one of the phones.

Seeing her approach, he said a quick good-bye and hung up. "How is he? I've been making arrangements for one of the finest heart men in the country to fly in." He paused as her stricken expression registered with him. "What's wrong?"

"Take me back to the hotel, please."

Ginnie cast a vacant glance around the elegant living room of their hotel suite. Her gaze stopped at a closet. The only thing that kept her from going to the closet to see if there was an extra blanket was the fact that she seriously doubted if a blanket would really help. She felt encased in ice.

Damien paced the room like a wild animal who sensed an impending attack but didn't know from which direction it would be coming. "For God's sake, talk to me, Ginnie. You haven't spoken a word since we left the hospital. You haven't even let me touch you. What's wrong? What happened?"

Shock had blocked coherent thought in the limo on the drive from the hospital to the hotel. A certain numbness had protected her from the pain she felt waiting to explode inside her. But nevertheless she had been totally aware of Damien, his muscular legs stretched out before him, his long-fingered hands resting on his knees, his left hand bearing the golden wedding band she had put there herself twenty-four hours earlier.

Unsure what it would do to her if she looked at him, she walked slowly to the window and gazed out toward the night lights of the San Francisco Bay. "Nathan said he tried to reach me last night, but couldn't."

His brow cleared as he realized what must have happened. "Oh, I'm sorry. I asked that the staff hold all calls until the next afternoon. It was our wedding night, and I—"

"It was you who took over Nathan's company."

"Nathan's company?" he said, puzzlement in his voice. "Camden Electronics? Yes."

"Why didn't you tell me?"

He shrugged. "I didn't think it was important."

She saw lights that indicated several boats were

out in the bay, moving over the dark water. How did those people on those boats get so lucky, she wondered, to be sailing over the water beneath the rising moon, with the wind in their hair and their hearts free of care? "You didn't think it was important that you were intent on stealing what a man had spent a lifetime building?"

"I didn't *steal* anything, Ginnie, and I don't understand why you're so fixated on the damned takeover. I paid a hell of a lot of money for the company, ensuring Nathan Camden an enormous profit, enough so that he can retire and never want for anything the rest of his life. Dammit, look at me!"

Her eyes remained on the lights of the boats.

He had never known such frustration. She had erected a wall between them, but he didn't know what the barrier was made of or how to get through it. "Ginnie . . . my men had almost completed the takeover when we met. After that, things took off very fast with us. Camden Electronics dropped right out of my mind."

"Your men," she said tonelessly. "You don't have to get so much as a drop of blood on your hands, do you?"

A growing fear and desperation propelled him across the room, where he grasped her arms and turned her to face him. "Ginnie, listen to me. Try to understand. Once I met you, you were the only thing I could think of. I know you're upset about Nathan's heart attack, and it's natural that you are. But he's survived the initial attack, and the doctors I spoke with said he's holding his own. The specialist I contacted will be here in a few hours.

Everything's going to be all right. Don't let this affect us."

"I can't divide my life up into compartments as you can, Damien. And I can't get past the fact that you could make love to me while at the same time systematically going about taking Nathan's company away from him. *Nathan*, the man who raised me as a daughter."

He raked his hand through his hair. "Dammit, Ginnie, Camden Electronics was just another company in a long line of companies for me. And what was happening was part of my work, not part of us."

"The owner was my *stepfather*, the only father I can remember."

"So why didn't he tell you?"

"Because he didn't know I knew you. And Michael didn't tell me because he naturally assumed I knew, as Marcus did." A sob broke from her. "I feel so stupid."

The sound of her sob wrenched at his heart. "Ginnie, let me take you to bed—"

She jerked away. "*No!*"

He held up his hands, as a man might do if he were surrendering. "I wouldn't do anything but hold you. You're tired. Everything has hit you at once. You need a good night's sleep. Tomorrow you'll have a better perspective."

"Perspective? *Perspective?*" She slowly shook her head. "What kind of man are you?"

"You should know. You know me better than anyone."

"No, no, I don't. I thought I did, but I don't."

"Then I'll tell you. I'm a man who loves you mor than himself."

"You don't know the meaning of love, Damien. She put her hand over her mouth, as if to form dam against the sounds of pain that were so clos to escaping. "I've got to get out of here, get awa from you." She snatched up her purse and bolte for the door.

Somehow Damien got there before her an blocked her exit. "Good Lord, Ginnie, where yo think you're going? It's close to midnight."

"I'm going somewhere where you're not." Sh reached around him and grasped the doorknob but once again he stopped her, putting a hand o her arm.

"You're my *wife*, Ginnie. You belong here with me.

She could feel hysteria building inside her. " you don't get out of my way, I'm going to star screaming, and I'm not sure I'll be able to stop."

"All right," he said gently, worriedly eyeing th lack of color in her face, "all right. Just tell m where you'll be."

"For tonight, I'll be at Nathan's house. After that I don't know."

It took every ounce of strength he possessed, bu he stepped away from the door.

Without looking at him again, she opened it an walk out.

And watching her, Damien felt as though hi soul had been sliced in two.

The next couple of days passed in a blur fo Ginnie. She spent her days at the hospital, an her nights in the house on Nob Hill where she had grown up. Nathan's struggle to improve was a painful, exhausting thing to watch. But she was at his bedside whenever the medical staff would allow, trying to encourage him with her presence and her love.

Damien stayed away from the hospital, but he called every day. He was obviously playing a waiting game with her, thinking that, given time, she would come to understand that she had overreacted. She lay awake nights wondering if she had. But she always reached the same conclusion. She had been too dazzled by him, too naive to see that he had no sense of humanity or compassion.

One morning, Ginnie woke up to the realization that Michael hadn't once come to see Nathan. He must still be very angry with her, she reflected. But the more she thought about it, the more puzzled she became. It was completely out of character for Michael to ignore Nathan when he was so ill. She picked up the phone, called the office, and asked for him.

"Ginnie, is that you? This is Mary."

"Mary, for heaven's sake, what are you doing answering Michael's phone?" Mary was Nathan's longtime secretary.

"With Mr. Camden in the hospital, and the new regime already here, there's not that much for me to do. Besides, this is my last week. I've put in my notice. With Mr. Camden gone, I might as well leave. I want nothing to do with that Averone group." She paused. "I'm sorry if I've offended you—I know you're married to the man—but that's just how I feel."

Ginnie sighed. "You didn't offend me, Mary. Would you please connect me to Michael?"

There was a silence on the line then. "Michael is in Sagrado Montanas. I thought you knew."

"No, I—Good heavens, Mary, what is he doing down there?" The morning paper had reported the fighting there had escalated.

"He was sent."

Ginnie pondered that for a moment. "By whom?"

"By your husband."

Ginnie hung up the phone and collapsed into the nearest chair. She felt as if she had stepped off the edge of the world the night she had met Damien, and there'd been no one there to catch her. She'd been falling ever since.

She stayed in the chair for a long time, trying to sort out what she should do. Her first instinct was to leave San Francisco and go back to the safety and security of her houseboat. Maybe there she could discover if there was any peace or sense left in her life. And she could still get up early every morning and make the drive into San Francisco, stay with Nathan until about two in the afternoon, then head back home. She'd also monitor the situation in Sagrado Montanas.

And most important, she could try to come to some decision about her marriage and her future.

Yes, she thought, she'd do that.

But first she had something else she needed to do.

There were people Ginnie had never seen before in the hallways of Camden Electronics. She walked straight past them and into Nathan's office. As Mary had told her, Damien was there, sitting in Nathan's chair, using Nathan's desk.

Damien's head jerked up and he saw her, standing before him, wearing her jeans and a long cable-knit sweater, with her hair a tousled mass around her face and shoulders and her eyes storm-filled.

She was furious, he thought, but he didn't care. It had been sheer hell staying away from her. And now, for whatever reason, *she had come to him.* She could yell at him, she could hit him, but at least she was here with him. Maybe this time he could make her understand.

He leaned back in his chair and drank in the sight of her. "Hello, Ginnie. It's good to see you again. I understand that Nathan is improving. I'm glad."

Seeing him again was every bit as hard as she had imagined. She no longer had the insulation of numbness. There was only the pain. She wanted to shout and rail at him. And suddenly she did. "Damn you, Damien. How could you?"

He exhaled a long breath. "You're still upset about your stepfather's company."

"Yes, dammit, I am! Plus, the one other little thing you've done. Minor really," she said with fierce sarcasm. "I'm sure sending a man into a revolution is something you manage to sandwich in quite nicely between lunch and a game of handball."

"Revolution? What are you talking about?"

"You're a dismal failure at playing stupid, Damien. Sagrado Montanas, that's what I'm talking about. You sent Michael into a country that's about to erupt. People should be *leaving* there, not going into it. Why in heaven's name did you do it? Were you that jealous?"

"No." He stood and walked around to the front of the desk. "First of all, it's not a revolution, only scattered rebel activity. And secondly, Straton was sent down there for one reason and one reason only. He was the best man for the job."

"I can't believe you are denying being jealous! You haven't been able to stand the thought of me and another man, no matter what the context, since Day One. Jealousy is a corrosive emotion, Damien. In biblical days King David sent Bathsheba's husband, Uriah, into battle, and Uriah was killed. Is that what you had in mind?"

"Of course not." He shook his head impatiently. "You're making too much of this. There have been no reported incidents where any civilian has been killed or even harmed down there. Besides which, we're on top of the situation. We've started an orderly evacuation of our employees. By this time next week, everyone will be safely back here."

"You still don't get it, do you? You don't understand what you've done. Because of this so-called love you have for me, you swept me away to New York and away from my life. Consequently, when you took Nathan's company away from him, I wasn't here to comfort him. When he learned I was marrying you, it was all too much for him. His heart couldn't take it." Her feelings of guilt were as strong as her anger, but for the moment she let her anger rein. "Now you've sent one of my oldest friends into danger because you were jealous."

Despair and desperation overwhelmed Damien as he searched for the words that would somehow make everything right again. "I never meant to hurt you. Don't you realize I would move mountains and destroy worlds to protect you?"

She wanted to cry, for Nathan, for Michael, but most of all for herself. The love of her life had turned out to be no more substantial than a pile of ashes. "And don't you realize you've done nothing *but* hurt me, Damien?"

He was stunned. He felt as if his legs had been cut out from under him. Despite all the ways he had tried to control the situation, he had failed. But he refused to believe he had lost her. "Ginnie—"

One of the men she had seen outside and not recognized hurried past her to Damien. "We've just learned that our offices in Sagrado Montanas have been stormed and occupied. Michael Straton has been taken hostage."

His gaze flew to Ginnie.

Without a word, she turned and walked out.

Damien swayed, took an unsteady step backward, and sank against the desk. The expression in Ginnie's eyes as she had looked at him had been one of agony and revulsion, and had seared him all the way to his soul. He didn't think he would ever get over it.

". . . the government assures us . . . under control . . . everything will be done to . . ."

He knew his assistant was trying to brief him on the situation in Sagrado Montanas, but his words seemed to come from a great distance. Ginnie, her face, her eyes, dominated his mind.

Everything he had done had gone wrong.

He had hurt her badly.

". . . Straton . . . no danger . . . returned soon."

Damien twisted around and grasped the picture of Ginnie that Nathan had kept on his desk. He stared at the picture, knowing from having studied it over the last few days that Ginnie had been on the beach when it had been taken. The camera had frozen a moment in time when her reddish-brown hair was flying around her, her green eyes were sparkling happily, and her soft, wide mouth was spread in laughter.

He stared hard, but in his mind all he could see was the pain on her face as she had looked when she had left the office. He had created that face.

Seven

The tears persisted, but Ginnie managed to make it back to Nathan's house without incident. Once there, she determinedly brushed the tears away. Falling apart was a luxury she couldn't afford now, she told herself. Her heart might be in pieces, but her mind was intact and she needed to use it to help Michael.

She knew Sagrado Montanas only as a visitor, but if sheer will signified anything, she was convinced she had a good chance of finding Michael.

It wasn't as if she thought she was possessed of any particular skills that would be helpful in a country about to light up like a Roman candle. In fact, she had no skills that would help her in a revolution-torn country, but then she didn't know anyone else who did either. And as far as she could tell, she was the only one who gave a damn whether Michael lived or died. That had to count for something.

She only had to get there.

It was to her advantage there was still some semblance of government control. Out of desire to have her accompany him whenever possible, Nathan had always seen to it that her travel papers to Sagrado Montanas were kept in order.

Theoretically, there would still be commercial flights in and out of the capital city; however, a quick call informed her that though seats were available into the country, she couldn't be assured of a seat out for either herself or Michael.

She paused and took stock of her financial situation. She was able to live comfortably because of a small trust fund left her by her mother and because of the money she made teaching. Unfortunately, her checking-account balance was low at the moment because she hadn't been teaching. And it took time to make large withdrawals from the trust fund. But there were other ways. . . .

The next morning she drew nearly all of the money out of her checking account and got a cash advance on her credit card. Then she headed for the airport and quite coolly set about using the power of her new married name: Mrs. Damien Averone. It worked. Within a very short time she had rented a private plane and had arranged for Damien to be billed. For a brief moment she felt a twinge of guilt, but she immediately banished the feeling.

She would pay Damien back as soon as she could, she reasoned. For now, though, expediency was the important thing, and the end would justify the means. Good Lord! Was she beginning to think like Damien?

The trip was long and tiring, and it was late at night when she arrived at El Presidente, the hotel where she and Nathan had always stayed.

"Miss Summers!" Enrique Matesanz, the dapper, dark-skinned manager of the hotel, hurried across the marbled floor toward her, an anxious expression on his face. "We weren't expecting you." His gaze darted behind her. "Is Mr. Camden with you?"

Her forced smile attempted to hide her weariness. "Hello, Enrique. No, Nathan didn't come on this trip."

Enrique wrung his hands, something she had never seen him do. From her previous visits she knew him to possess the urbanity and poise one would expect from a manager of an old and respected hotel. Now worry dominated his distinguished face.

"Señorita, you should know it is always a joy to see you, but you really shouldn't be here at this time. There is such danger in my country now."

She cast a look around the lobby of the charming, elegant, old world-style hotel. "That's what I've heard. But on my way in from the airport, I didn't see any signs of trouble, though I did see plenty of soldiers. And it looks as if things are running normally here."

He nodded, following her gaze, taking in his domain with a critical eye. "We're trying to maintain our standards. Naturally, most of the foreign press who are in the country are staying here. And tomorrow evening, the government is holding a ball here, staged to show there is nothing to worry about and they are still in control."

"They are, aren't they?"

He shrugged. "They say so, but the rumblings from the revolutionaries up in the mountains are strong. They come down and make lightning raids, and so far the government has been able to do nothing."

"One of the rebels' lightning raids is why I'm here. I received word that they have taken Michael Straton hostage. I've come to see what I can do about finding him. He was staying here, wasn't he?"

"Sí, Sí, he was, but no one has seen him in two days." His hands twisted together. "Señorita Summers, I hope you don't mind my saying this, but you really shouldn't have come."

"I'm sure you're right, but nevertheless I seem to be here, don't I? And I've got my fingers crossed that you have a room for me, plus another one for my pilot. He stayed behind at the airport to secure the plane, but he'll be along shortly."

"Of course, señorita, and please forgive me for being less than gracious. It is just that these are difficult times. If I can be of any help in assisting you in your search for Mr. Straton, please let me know."

"There is something . . . I'll need a car and a reliable driver, first thing in the morning."

"Sí, señorita. And how would you like to handle the billing while you are with us?" His dark brows lifted in inquiry, his demeanor now changed from that of a concerned acquaintance to manager of a grand hotel. Business, after all, was business. "Señor Straton told me Camden Electronics is under new ownership."

She sighed. She had hoped he would assume that the billing would be handled as it always had been. She didn't like to lie, even in spirit. "I'm sorry I haven't mentioned this before, but perhaps you should know. I am now Señora Averone. My husband, Damien Averone, is the new owner of Camden Electronics. The bill should go to the company as it always has."

His eyes lit up. "Excellent, *señora*. Excellent. And please allow me to wish you all good wishes."

Damien's name magically opened doors for her, she reflected, and for a brief, incautious period of time, she had opened the door of her heart to him. Her hand went to the back of her neck and rubbed. "Thank you. Now if you don't mind, I'd like to go to my room."

"*Sí, señora*. Right this way."

Ginnie was so tired, she had barely undressed before she collapsed onto the bed and fell instantly asleep. She slept hard, and the next morning she awoke refreshed and determined.

She knew exactly where she wanted to go. She just wasn't sure what she'd find once she got there. She gave the driver Julio Casado's address, which was on the outskirts of the city, sat back in the seat, and crossed her fingers that he would be there.

Julio Casado had been born and raised in Sagrado Montanas and was a longtime employee of Camden Electronics. She and Nathan had been in his home several times as dinner guests. It was her hope that he would be able to help her.

Her heart lightened considerably as they drove. She saw no signs anywhere of fighting. And when they pulled up in front of Julio's house, the modest white stucco structure looked the same as when she had last seen it. Its yard was neatly manicured and enclosed by a white wrought-iron fence. Picturesque blue shutters framed the windows, and colorful flowering plants spilled out of red clay pots that sat on the tiled patio.

At her knock, Julio, a tall, darkly handsome man, appeared in the doorway, a guarded expression on his face. But the minute he saw her, his expression changed to astonishment. "*Señorita* Ginnie!" He threw a quick glance up and down the street, then out at the car and her driver. "What are you doing here? You should not be here."

She grinned ruefully. "So I understand, but Michael is missing, and I had to come. Can I talk with you?"

"Yes, of course." With a last look up and down the street, he waved her inside to a comfortable living room. "I don't recognize your driver. How did you find him?"

"The manager of the hotel recommended him. His name is Carlos. Julio, are you alone here?"

"*Sí.* I've sent my family away. The trouble, it is coming."

"But everything seems so"—she shrugged her shoulders—"normal."

"Things are normal only on the surface. My country is about to be split apart, and I am very much afraid."

"Then why are you still here?"

"I'm going to be needed," he said.

"Oh, Julio . . ." As nothing else had, his simple statement impressed upon her the tragedy and enormity of what was about to happen. "Your beautiful country."

"Sí. My beautiful country."

She touched a sympathetic hand to his arm, then straightened. "Could we sit down? I need to ask you a few questions."

"Sí, of course." He indicated the sofa, waited until she had taken a seat, then dropped down into a chair across from her.

She leaned forward. "Julio, do you have any idea where Michael is?"

"No, *señorita*, I don't. Unfortunately, the fact that the factory of Camden Electronics is located just outside the city made it a perfect target for the revolutionaries. We weren't prepared, and there was much panic. A lot of the workers were able to escape into the hills. I was able to help some of the Americans get out and reach their embassy. From there, most of them have already been flown back to the States. But I never saw Michael."

"Think hard. Do you have any contacts with anyone who might be able to help me?"

After a long silence he said slowly, "Sí. I have not thought of it before, but there is a man. You are staying at the hotel, are you not?"

"Yes."

"The man is named Gerardo Padilla. He is a low-ranking officer in the army, and a man who walks sometimes on one side of the fence, sometimes on the other. I know from experience he can be bribed." He paused. "I assume you have brought money."

"Some. I hope it is enough."

"At this time, American dollars of any amount will be much in demand for those with less than honorable intentions toward our country. American dollars will buy much on the black market. They will also provide a way out of here." He shrugged. "I don't know what Padilla will be thinking or planning, but let me try to find him. If I do, and if he says he has information, I'll have him ask you to dance with him at the ball tonight."

"Ball?" she asked, surprised. "I'm not going to the ball."

"It would be the safest place for you to meet this man, believe me, and an invitation for you to the ball should be no problem. And no one would be suspicious of a lovely woman dancing with an officer at a party. Now"—he held up a warning finger—"there is a man you must stay away from at all costs tonight. His name is Colonel Amadis Zurdo, and he is Padilla's superior in the army. It is rumored that the colonel is affiliated with the rebels. Padilla is small change compared to this man. This man has access to many levels of knowledge, and should be regarded as very dangerous."

"All right, I'll try to remember that. And thank you for the warning. Now suppose Padilla is able to tell me where Michael is. Can you help me rescue him?"

Regret tinged his expression as he shook his head. "I will help you as much as I can, but I have already been assigned to duty by my government. I am only waiting for my orders."

She nodded, understanding. "Thank you, Julio. And may God be with you."

"And with you, Señorita Ginnie."

Ginnie smiled at the young officer with whom she was dancing and tried not to think about how badly her feet were hurting her. How could she have anticipated having to attend a formal ball when she had hurriedly packed for this trip? She'd stuffed only a few toiletries, an extra pair of jeans, and several tops into a duffel bag yesterday. As a result, she had had to pay a quick visit to one of the boutiques in the hotel this afternoon and had made yet more charges to Damien's account—a sequined and beaded black floor-length sheath she would probably never wear again and matching shoes that were pinching her toes and rubbing a blister on her heels.

The young officer had a glint of ardor in his eyes as he beamed down at her. "You are the most lovely of all the women here tonight, *señorita.* I am the envy of my friends."

"*Señora,*" she said, automatically reaching for the protection of marriage, then Damien's name. "I am Señora Averone." She was *using* Damien again, she thought, and without his knowledge. She felt a pang in the region of her heart and wondered why. After all, he deserved whatever she did to him. Didn't he?

The officer's face fell, but he rallied gallantly. "*Señora,* I still feel the most fortunate of men to be dancing with you."

"That's very kind of you to say," she said absently. *Where* was this Gerardo Padilla? she wondered. She had thought she might be easier to find if she were out on the dance floor rather than stuck at a table in a corner somewhere. But her present partner was the sixth young man with whom she had danced, and her feet were giving out.

Suddenly, she saw a man across the room, and her heart skipped a beat. For a flash of an instant she was reminded of Damien. Something about the proud way he held his head and the wide line of his shoulders. But no, the man was older and without the magnetism Damien possessed.

Wondering why she felt disappointed, she gazed around the glittering room. Beneath the merriment the tension was palpable. If the ball had been intended to allay people's fears, then it was not succeeding very well, she concluded as the orchestra brought the song to an end. The young officer released her, and they both politely applauded.

"May I have this dance, *señorita*?"

Ginnie pasted another smile on her face and wearily turned. Her gaze went first to the face of the officer standing in front of her and the small crescent-shaped scar above his left brow. Then she glanced at his name tag. *Padilla.* Her gaze flew back to his face. "I'd be delighted."

They danced in silence for more than a minute before Ginnie's impatience got the better of her. "I gather Julio Casado spoke with you?"

"*Sí, señorita,*" Padilla said, alertly scanning the ballroom. "And he said you had money."

"Only for the right information. I'm interested in finding Camden Electronics employee Michael

Straton. The rebels took him, and I need to know where they are holding him. Can you help me?"

"*Sí*, and if we can work out a deal, I will—" He stiffened. "*Dios*! It is Zurdo!"

"Zurdo?" The name didn't register with her at first. She glanced blankly over her shoulder in the direction in which Padilla was staring. A tall, swarthy man in an officer's uniform that bore a colonel's insignia was leaning against one of the marble columns and watching her and Padilla with a degree of interest that Ginnie found extremely ominous. Zurdo, the man she was supposed to avoid.

Padilla jerked away from her. "I must go."

"No, wait, you've got to help me. I'll pay you any sum you can name." His sudden stillness told her she had his attention. "I don't have it all with me, but within twenty-four hours after I have Michael back in the States, I will wire it to you."

He dislodged her grip from him. "I don't have time for jokes, *señorita*. Meet me in the alley behind the hotel in three hours. But only come if you have a large sum of money, because that is what it is going to take to free your friend."

Ginnie made a sound of frustration as she watched him disappear into the crowd.

"Dance, *señora*?"

She almost groaned. Her feet were killing her, and the heavily beaded gown was weighing her down. "No—"

A masculine hand grasped hers, and she was swung around until she came up against a broad chest. Then an arm slid around her and she was dancing. Astonished, she looked up into golden-brown eyes and a compellingly rugged face and felt a heated shock all the way to her toes.

"*Damien!*"

"Hello, Ginnie."

He was careful to keep his voice free of any inflection, but he could do nothing about the pain he felt inside. He was holding her again, but they were in the middle of a room filled with over two hundred people. And in a moment, he knew, as soon as she had had time to get over her surprise, he was going to see anger and hate in her eyes. He hadn't known he could love anyone with the depth he loved her until she had come into his life. But in trying to hold on to her, he had lost her. And now he could only try to keep her safe.

"You look incredibly beautiful tonight," he murmured.

The hunger in his gaze sent a warmth skittering through her. It was the feeling she had known every time she laid eyes on him. "What are you doing here? How did you find me?"

"You leased a private jet, using my name. Didn't you think they'd check with me?"

She almost cursed aloud. How could she have been so stupid? She had had no form of identification to show them, only her word that she was Mrs. Damien Averone. "If they checked with you, you could have stopped me. Why didn't you?"

He shook his head. "You would have found another way, and by giving my okay, I knew your schedule. My plane was fifteen minutes behind yours."

She felt the old, familiar cold seep into her and tried to free herself, but his hold on her only tightened. "*Dammit*, Damien. After all that's happened, you're still trying to control me! I *left* you. Don't you understand? I don't want to be around you or with you. Not back home. Not here."

"I'm sorry about that, but I couldn't let you come down here by yourself, Ginnie." His voice was quiet and calm, though a muscle flicked incessantly along his jawline. "What I'd really like is for you to leave and go back home."

He was different, she suddenly realized. His intensity had turned inward, and he was quietly burning up inside. But then, she, too, had changed. From somewhere she had gained more self-confidence. "What you'd like doesn't interest me anymore. I'm staying."

"That's what I thought you'd say. And as long as you're here, I'll be here."

"Damien—"

"Excuse me." A deep, heavily accented voice interrupted her. "I'd like to introduce myself. I am Colonel Amadis Zurdo."

Damien felt Ginnie freeze and didn't have to ask why. Bells of alarm were also going off in him. Nevertheless, he turned toward the man and held out his hand. "I'm Damien Averone."

"Yes, I know," said Zurdo, taking Damien's hand. "Your picture ran in our paper with an article stating you are the new owner of Camden Electronics. The people of Sagrado Montanas have always been proud of the Camden Electronics factory here. It has brought many jobs to us, and is a symbol of our friendship with the American people."

The man was oily smooth, Damien concluded.

And as dangerous as a snake. "Then why do you suppose the revolutionaries swept through it the other day with their guns blazing?"

The colonel shrugged, a universal gesture that in his case conveyed lack of concern. "A show of strength and intent perhaps. At any rate, no one was hurt."

"We don't know that," Ginnie blurted out. Zurdo's eyes narrowed on her, but Damien laid a light, almost reassuring hand on her shoulder. Whatever his intent, she was able to gather her composure. "A friend of mine was taken that day and has not been heard from since. Michael Straton."

"Mr. Straton. Yes," Zurdo said thoughtfully, as if he were recalling something distant and only mildly interesting. "On that day he was the most important American in our country, except for the ambassador, who, of course, is protected by a squad of United States Marines." The colonel's dark head turned to Damien. "I would think that now, Mr. Averone, *you* would be the most important American. You *and* the lovely Miss Summers."

The calculation in the colonel's expression and the glint of avarice in his eyes were unmistakable. Damien bit back the words that would contradict Zurdo and proclaim Ginnie his wife. "As I'm sure you can understand, we are very worried about Mr. Straton. We have not heard any word or received a ransom note."

"I can almost assure you, money will be requested."

"Requested, Colonel? That is a very polite term

for what is most definitely the barbaric act of kidnapping."

Zurdo's teeth showed very white as he smiled. "You are right, of course, *señor*. My English is sometimes not very good."

Damien let the lie pass. "I don't suppose you know of Mr. Straton's whereabouts."

"No, I'm afraid not." His lips moved, making his smile even more of a parody, and he held up a finger as if an idea had just occurred to him. "Perhaps your United States embassy can be of help."

Cute, Damien thought. Real cute, the bastard. "Thank you so much for the suggestion. Now if you'll excuse us, it's time we retired."

With the grin still pasted on his face, the colonel bowed. "I will see you again, I'm sure."

It was with relief that Ginnie felt Damien fasten long, slim fingers around her elbow and begin to guide her from the ballroom. Careful to keep her voice pitched low, she said, "Julio warned me to be cautious of that man."

"Julio?"

"A friend and employee of Camden Electronics here."

They didn't speak again until they reached her room. She wasn't anxious to be alone with him. In fact, she had hoped she would never have to see him again. It would have been so much easier that way. Never to have to feel the way her body came to life when he was near. Never to have to smell his scent or look at his lips and remember . . . But she knew, much as she would like it to happen, he wasn't simply going to go away. He had to be dealt with—and quickly—because she still had to prepare for her meeting with Padilla.

In her room Damien made a fast tour, checking that they were alone and that the windows were locked. He came back to her just in time to see her strip off her shoes and throw them into the wastepaper basket. He raised his eyebrows, but made no comment about her action. "What exactly did this Julio tell you about Zurdo?"

She sank down onto the bed and began to massage her feet. "That he is rumored to be with the revolutionaries."

"That figures. He came across to me as a very hungry, ambitious man."

Remembering the almost malevolent way Zurdo had looked at them both, Ginnie shuddered. "Damien, you're in danger down here. If the revolutionaries think Michael has worth as a hostage, they must be salivating over the prospect of nabbing you."

"Funny, I was just having similar thoughts about you. Especially if it gets out that you're my wife. At that point, it's bound to occur to them that I'd pay a king's ransom to get you back."

"Yes," she said slowly, "I guess that is what they'd think." Funny, she thought. They had been together now for almost thirty minutes, yet he hadn't pleaded with her to take him back, and he hadn't given her any protestations of love as she might have expected him to do. But she had no doubt that he *would* pay a king's ransom for her. "Unfortunately, I've told a few people that we're married—the manager of the hotel, Julio, someone I danced with—but rest assured,

I won't tell anyone else. Just go home, Damien. I'll be fine."

"I can't, Ginnie."

"Yes, you can. Listen to me. The only reason you flew down here was because you were concerned for my safety. But I don't want or need you. I've already made some useful contacts. And as long as people don't know that I'm your wife, I'll be safe." She stopped because suddenly she noticed something in his eyes, something she had never seen in them before. *Sadness.*

"I know you will be," he said, "because I intend to keep you that way." He gave her a brief smile bereft of humor or happiness and walked toward the door.

They were *both* miserably unhappy, she realized. And Nathan was in the hospital, and Michael was God knew where.

How had their lives become so tangled when it had started so simply and so naturally with a kiss on the beach?

His hand closed around the doorknob, but he turned and looked back at her. "You really don't know everything you think you do. You believe you're the only reason I'm here. You also believe you're the only one who cares whether Michael gets out of this country alive or not, and that it was up to you to come and try to rescue him because no one else would. But the real fact is, you walked out of my office without bothering to find out what I intended to do about Michael's situation." He paused as if he were about to say something else, but then seemed to change his mind. "Call me if you need me, but try to get some sleep."

Alone, Ginnie was shaken by his words. It had never once occurred to her that he would make any attempt to rescue Michael. Indeed, she had accused him of sending Michael into the country for just this end—all motivated by the obsessive jealousy she'd likened to David's for Bathsheba. Was it possible that she had judged him prematurely and too harshly?

With a heavy heart she unzipped the black beaded dress and reached for her jeans.

Clutching her purse to her chest, Ginnie swallowed hard and entered the long, dark alley. The music that came from the ballroom had a distant, hollow sound to it, and vied with the pounding in her ears. She tried to imagine herself still there with the other guests, safe in the midst of the dancing and forced joviality. It didn't work. She was scared to death.

The alley was filled with crazily shaped, menacing shadows. As she passed a group of trash cans, she heard something skitter behind them and hurried her step. Where was Padilla? she wondered frantically. How deep was she going to have to go into the alley before he made contact with her? Was he even going to show up?

She walked farther, once accidentally kicking an empty soft-drink can and sending it rolling noisily away. She viewed each doorway she passed as a potential ambush, each shadow as a potential assassin. She should have told Damien where she was going, she thought, her nerves stretched out like thin wire. At the least, she should have left a note. She should have—

One of the shadows near her moved. Her heart nearly stopped. Then she heard a fierce whisper.

"Here I am. Did you bring the money?"

"Do you have the information I need?"

"I do not have time to play games, *señorita*. Zurdo saw us together and is after me. The American is at a base camp in the foothills of the mountains. I have drawn a map to show you the exact location. Give me the money, and I will give you the map."

She opened her purse and pulled out a stack of bills she'd counted in her hotel room and banded with a rubber band. She had several hundred dollars tucked away in her purse. "I'll give you partial payment now of more than a thousand dollars and the rest when I have the map in my hand and assurances it is authentic and will lead me to Michael."

"American dollars?"

"Yes, all I have."

"It had better be a lot, lady." With angry, jerky movements he thrust a folded piece of paper into her hands and snatched the money she held toward him.

"Do you guarantee this information?"

He snarled in response, shook his head yes, and demanded, "Give me the rest of the money."

"This is all I have," she said, handing him the second half of the bills she had allocated for him. "That's two thousand dollars in all. Take it."

"Two thousand! You are lying! You *must* have more. You're rich!" With eyes that gleamed wildly in the dim light, he grabbed her purse from her and started tearing through it.

Her only thought was that she couldn't let him have the only money she had left. She was going to need it for supplies. She reached out for the purse. "You can't have that! It's mine!" She kicked out at his leg, making contact.

A rain of deafening gunfire hit the wall behind them. Padilla made a funny sound and fell backward. Then all the breath was pushed from her body as she was knocked to the ground and a heavy weight came down on top of her. She blinked and slowly focused on the face above hers. *Damien's* face.

Bullets hit the metal of the trash cans and dug into the ground around them. Damien dragged her to the nearest doorway, opened the door, pushed her inside, and closed the door after them. Ginnie rubbed at her eyes. They were in a small, dark hallway. He didn't say anything, but she could feel the heat of his body and thought she could hear the pounding of his heart. Or was that hers?

Outside, the gunfire continued for what seemed to her an eternity but reason told her was probably only seconds. Then there was silence.

"Damien—"

His hand came over her mouth, quieting her. A few more minutes passed. Finally, he whispered, "Wait here."

Before she could protest, he was out the door. Trembling uncontrollably, she wrapped her arms around her drawn-up knees. They were in a foreign country that was in the early throes of violent revolution, and they might very well die here. Oh, Lord. If something happened to Damien . . . She started to pray.

Then he was back.

"The man you were meeting with is dead." He thrust her purse at her and gripped her arm. "Let's get out of here."

"Wait, he's got my money!"

"The money is torn to pieces and covered in blood, Ginnie."

Damien handed her a glass filled with whiskey from the hotel bar. "Drink."

She was on the bed with a blanket wrapped around her, all Damien's doing. And she hated whiskey, but she had never in her life felt less like arguing. She took a sip, welcoming the burning sensation as the liquor slid down her throat and into her stomach.

Slowly, her eyes focused on him. He had his own glass of whiskey. She stared at his hand. It was shaking. "You saved my life, Damien."

His expression was bleak. "Thank God." He knocked back a hefty amount of the whiskey.

"How did you know—?"

"My room's next door. I heard you leave, and I followed. What in the hell did you think you were doing?"

"I was buying information." Suddenly, she looked down at her left hand and saw that she still clutched the map. "And I got it!" She spread open the sheet of paper and saw a roughly drawn map.

"Look! It's a map of a base camp where they're holding Michael."

He took the paper from her and studied it. "If that man was being honest with you, then this will go a long way toward helping me get Michael for you."

"*You?*"

"Yes, me," he said, his tone grim. "It's my fault Michael's here. I'll be the one to get him out. You've risked your life for the last time, if I can help it." He looked at his watch. "It's late. You don't have any more secret meetings you have to go to, do you?"

Wearily, she shook her head. "No, but I'm glad I went to that one."

"Yeah, I'm thrilled too. I loved watching you almost get killed."

"Damien—"

With a pained expression he held up a hand. "I'm sorry. I shouldn't have said that. It's just that I don't think I'll ever get over the fear I felt when I saw you and that man—" He shook his head. "Never mind. Try to get some sleep."

"I'm not sure I can."

He hesitated. "If it would help you, I could stay with you, just until you fall asleep. I could sit over in the chair."

She glanced at the chair he indicated. It didn't look very comfortable for a man his size. Yet she welcomed the idea of his staying with her. No matter what had gone before between the two of them, his presence was reassuring to her. In fact, if he had said he would sleep beside her on the bed, she would have agreed. But he hadn't, and she couldn't ask him. "If you don't mind, I think it would help."

She watched as he folded his long frame into the chair. "Damien?"

"Yes?"

"Thank you for saving my life."

From across the room she saw his eyes darken. "You're welcome."

She waited, but he didn't say anything else. Exhausted and troubled, she curled up like a child beneath the blanket. And soon she was sound asleep.

Eight

"Wake up, Ginnie. Wake up."

She slowly opened her eyes, and Damien's face swam into soft focus. And for a moment in that dreamworld of half sleep, half wakefulness, she believed things were all right between them. She loved him, and he loved her. And he was about to take her into his arms and make love to her.

"Ginnie, the rebels are in the city. There's fighting everywhere."

"What?" She sat up and brushed the hair from her eyes, as if it would clear the dreams from her mind. She saw Damien sitting at the edge of the bed, one hand placed on the opposite side of her legs, supporting his weight. Then she heard the sound of distant guns. "When did it start?"

"Not too long ago. I heard the reporters knocking on doors, waking each other up. They nearly broke their necks trying to get outside and cover it." He paused. "Ginnie, the subject hasn't come up before now, but Max is here, or rather, he's at the airport. He flew me in."

Her eyes widened. "Max?"

He grinned. "He can fly anything that has wings and some things that don't. Flying is one of his passions. Anyway, while I've been with you, Max has been busy tapping into the black market. He bought a car for us and has stocked it with everything from medical supplies to guns. After you fell asleep, I made my way to the airport, got the car, and drove it back here. It's outside now, and we need to leave as soon as we can."

She pressed a hand to her forehead. "Damien, you've been awake all night. I just woke up. You're going too fast for me. Where are we going?"

"Away from the fighting. From what I can make out, the rebels are hitting the military installations first."

"Good Lord, the *airport*!"

"Don't worry. The army will fight tooth and nail to keep it secure. It's their lifeline to the outside world."

She worriedly gnawed on her lower lip. "I hope they're successful, because it's our lifeline too. We both have planes there."

"Yeah, and by the way, is your pilot staying here?" At her nod he said, "Call him and tell him to try to make his way to the airport and take as many Americans and other foreigners with him as the plane will carry. That way, if things get too dicey, he can always fly them out of here. And we'll still have Max."

"Okay, but what's the urge to get away from the hotel? Don't you think it's safe? The press is staying here. I would think the rebels would want to get their message out to the world."

"Yeah, but they're going to want to be in charge of what's being transmitted, plus, if they're thinking— and I'm sure they are—they'll put all Americans and foreigners under house arrest, just in case they need some sort of leverage."

"What kind of resistance are they meeting?"

"Impossible to tell. The radio is government-controlled, so all we'll hear is propaganda. Ginnie, we can't take chances."

"I agree." She thought for a moment. "We've got to get to Michael as fast as we can before the rebels' power is solidified. Wait a minute, I've just thought of something. We can go to Julio's house. He probably won't be there, but we should be able to get in, and we'll be safe there, at least for a little while."

"Do you remember the directions?"

She nodded. "I think so. And I'm pretty sure the house isn't near any strategic installation."

"Good, then get your things together, and while you're doing that and contacting your pilot, I'm going to try to get in touch with Zurdo."

The man's name stopped her cold and sent chills down her spine. "Why?"

"Because I want him to meet us in the hotel lobby within the hour. I want to try to get him to help us get Michael."

"Help us? Are you crazy? We can't trust Zurdo!"

"You're right. Besides ourselves, Max is the only other person in this whole damned country we can trust. But that doesn't mean we can eliminate the rest of the population as people who might help us."

"Yes, but *Zurdo*."

"Ginnie, I've dealt with hundreds of Zurdos in my life. His type is universal, and the key to him is simple. He's out for himself. He's standing with one foot in each camp at the moment, waiting to see the outcome. And he'll leave the loser without a qualm. He wants power, and I understand him. Until recently, there was more of him in me than I care to admit."

"Until recently?"

He reached out a hand to her hair, but then pulled back before he could touch her. "I used to look at you and all I could think about was how I could make you mine and bind you to me so that you'd never leave me. It was I, I, I, and my way blew up in my face. Now I have no other option but to look at you and ask myself how I can help you get whatever it is that you want. What is it, Ginnie?"

For a moment she became lost in the golden brown of his eyes. *What did she want?* She moistened her suddenly dry lips. "Why, I want Michael home safely. Of course."

"Then I'm going to get him for you," he said softly.

Ginnie stood by Damien's side in the lobby of the hotel, her duffel bag at her feet. Overnight, the normally gracious pace of the hotel had disappeared. Members of the press came in and out, manning every available phone as they called in their stories to the States. Enrique hurried here and there, aiding his guests, answering their questions. Tourists stood by their suitcases, waiting for armed transport to the airport. A dog ran loose through the lobby.

Suddenly, Colonel Zurdo was striding toward them, cutting a path through the activity. Dressed in an immaculate set of battle fatigues and wearing a side arm strapped to his hip, he had left four guards out in front of the hotel, she noted.

The colonel came to a smart stop in front of them and nodded. "*Señor. Señora.* When we met, you did not tell me that congratulations were in order, though, I understand, you do prefer separate rooms."

"We are separated," said Damien, silently cursing that the news was out.

Ginnie clasped her hands together and tried to look unperturbed. But silently she was berating herself. If she hadn't been so quick to use Damien's name to protect herself . . .

"What a pity," Zurdo murmured, "though it does seem you are together now." He flicked a glance to the bags at their feet. "I hope you're not leaving us. I'm afraid your safety could not be guaranteed if you did."

"There's no need for you to worry about us, Colonel. I know you must be busy."

"Yes, I am, but I was intrigued. Over the phone you said you had a matter of great importance to discuss with me."

"I said that," Damien agreed. "I also said that, financially, it would be in your best interest to come here."

Black eyes snapped impatiently. "Well? As you can see, I am here."

"I'd like you to arrange Michael Straton's release."

The colonel's eyebrows lifted into sharp peaks. "Are you mad? A revolution has just broken out. Fighting is everywhere. I don't have time for this nonsense."

"I'm well aware that your time is at a premium. Especially since the uniform you're wearing is reversible."

His eyes narrowed until they were almost slits. "I hope, Señor Averone, for your sake, that you are not implying what I think you are."

Damien smiled. "What I'm doing is suggesting that a revolution can become very tiring, very fast, and in some cases, even hazardous to your health, no matter what side you're on, and that two hundred thousand dollars in American cash would oil your way out of here to some nice comfortable beach house in another country where there is no fighting. Then after the winner is declared and you decide you'd like to come back, the money would give you the clout to buy your way to a position you desire."

The colonel's gaze flicked to Ginnie, then back to Damien. "This is all very interesting, but what makes you think that I know the whereabouts of Mr. Straton?"

A glance at Damien showed Ginnie he was still smiling. He was actually enjoying himself, she realized, amazed.

"Actually, I'm sure you do know. But the beauty of this whole deal is that we don't need you to tell us. We know where he is. All we're asking you to do is act as middleman. Make contact with the people guarding him, decide on what percentage of the money you're going to give them, and then deliver Michael to us at an appointed time and place subject to my approval."

The colonel rocked back on his heels, his expression assessing. "I will think on this. Where can I reach you with my decision?"

Damien's smile grew wider. "I'm not sure where we're going to be. I suggest a meeting this evening at ten o'clock at the old power station on the edge of town. Come alone, and I'll do the same."

"You know this place, Señor Averone?"

"I saw it on a map. Is it a deal?"

The colonel looked back at Ginnie. "I will see what I can do."

Her skin crawled as she felt his gaze on her. No matter what he agreed to, she thought, he meant her and Damien harm. Damien's next words affirmed that he was thinking the same thing.

"And, Zurdo, just so you'll know . . . I don't have the money with me now, and I won't have the money with me this evening."

Quick as a flash of lightning, Zurdo's gaze returned to Damien. "What's to prevent me from taking you both into, oh, shall we say, protective custody, right now? I'm sure there are people who would pay much more to get you back than the two hundred thousand dollars you are currently offering me for Straton."

"Maybe. But this country is closing down fast. It might take you weeks to get in touch with anyone in the States, and longer than that to get the money. But if you do things my way, you'll have two hundred thousand dollars in your hand in less than twenty-four hours."

The colonel smiled. "You make a very persuasive argument, Señor Averone."

As they drove along the roads that led to Julio's, Ginnie could hear the booming of guns, some sounding nearer than others. And in the distance she could see fire where part of the city burned.

She had an almost irresistible urge to slide along the seat to be nearer to Damien, but she resisted. He had his hands full, as he concentrated on steering around the people who were walking along the roads, trying to get out of the city. His task was much more important than comforting and reassuring her.

Besides, she reminded herself, just because she and Damien were working together to rescue Michael now didn't change what had gone before. Their marriage was over. And she ought to know. *She* had ended it.

"This has always been such a beautiful city," she murmured, her gaze on yet another distant fire. "I feel so badly for the people."

"I know, but hopefully they'll eventually be able to rebuild."

"Hopefully," she murmured, agreeing with him. "There's always been so much that's good about this country. It's why, years ago when the government came to America seeking trade and money, Nathan agreed to build a factory here. The arrangement benefited everyone."

Damien nodded. "The factory was a wise deci-

sion on Nathan's part. I thought so at the time I
initially looked over the company. And of course
there was no way Nathan could foresee this." His
hands tightened on the wheel as he steered the car
around a huge pothole.

Troubled, she watched him. "Damien, how are
you going to get your hands on two hundred
thousand dollars?"

"I brought it with me. As soon as I found out
what you were up to, I got the cash. Max is taking
care of it for now."

"All I could manage was twenty-five-hundred
dollars."

He glanced at her, a half-grin on his face. "I'm
surprised you didn't try to use my name to get a
larger sum."

"I didn't think of it," she admitted, then paused.
"I plan to pay you back, Damien, every cent."

For a moment the old possessiveness flared.
"Don't be silly. You're my wife." He fell abruptly
silent, then he slowly smiled. "Besides, admit it.
You enjoyed sticking me with what you thought
was an outrageous bill for the charter of the
plane."

She chuckled. "And don't forget the hotel bill
and that dress."

"The dress was definitely worth it. You were a
knockout in it."

His compliment pleased her, but she made a
face. "The shoes weren't worth it."

"I noticed you didn't think much of them."

"Maybe the maid will be able to get some use out
of them. I left the dress for her too." She laughed at

herself. "So much for fashion shopping in this country."

"You're ducking my question, Ginnie."

"Okay, okay, I admit that I enjoyed billing you for everything. A little." She thought for a moment. "At the time, I thought you deserved it."

"At the time?"

"As I said, I plan to pay you back."

"No—"

"Yes. And while we're admitting things, am I imagining it or are you actually having fun? You certainly seemed to be enjoying yourself back there with Zurdo."

He grimaced self-deprecatingly. "The thing of it is, if I were back in New York with my power base around me, I could have squashed someone like Zurdo with one halfhearted swat. Here, the power I've built up over the years means nothing. In fact, here, a mere colonel has more power than I do. And so I have to defeat him with my wits. If you were safe at home on your houseboat and Michael were out of danger, I would be having a great time. As it is, I'm too worried about you."

"Maybe, but you were still, most definitely, enjoying yourself back there with him."

He threw another glance her way, surprising her with a slight twinkle in his eye. "A little," he said.

And she was further surprised when she grinned back at him.

Julio's little house was deserted, as she had expected. What she hadn't expected was that it would be boarded up.

"By any chance, do you think one of Max's black-market purchases was a crowbar?" she asked, as Damien pulled the car around to the back of the house so that it wouldn't be seen from the road.

"I wouldn't be at all surprised. At any rate, I'm sure we'll find something we can use."

Working together, they managed to pry loose a few of the boards away from the window. As for the window, there was nothing for it but to break it.

Ginnie scrambled in, and Damien followed, two pistols tucked into the waistband of his jeans and an automatic rifle in his hands. After he was inside, he carefully pulled the boards back against the window so that from a distance it would look as if the whole house were still boarded up.

"That window is one more bill I'll have to pay," Ginnie murmured.

Damien came up beside her. "Another bill we'll pay together, okay?"

She nodded. "Okay." It seemed silly to quibble about who was going to pay for what when they were surrounded by danger and didn't know whether Michael was alive or dead.

She glanced around the main room. Had it been only yesterday morning when she and Julio had sat in this room? She had been so intent on trying to get some sort of information that would help her find Michael that she hadn't noticed much of her surroundings then. Now she saw the little rocking horse in the corner. An unfinished afghan in a basket by the couch. A baby's rattle on the coffee table. Closing her eyes, she said a silent prayer that the little boy who owned the rocking horse got to ride him again. And that the wife and mother was able to finish her afghan. And that the baby didn't miss her rattle too much. And that the father was able to come home safely and be reunited with his family.

"Don't worry," Damien said softly. "You and Michael are going to get home safely. I promise."

He had misinterpreted her silence, she thought, and she felt too saddened to explain. "Of course we are," she said brightly. "And you are too. Now, do you suppose we'll be lucky enough to find any food here? I can't remember the last time I ate, and I'm starving."

"I am, too, now that you mention it," he said, relieved her moody silence had been broken.

She looked at him in surprise. "That's a switch."

"Yes, well, I've never been in the middle of a revolution before. I'm finding it's doing amazing things to my appetite." He grinned. "Let's go check out the kitchen."

The kitchen, like the other rooms of the house, had boards over its windows and its curtains drawn, giving the false feeling that it was dusk outside. The gas stove was working. "We'll have hot water for a quick shower if we want," Damien said. "But I don't think we'd better do any cooking. We don't know how the stove is vented, and the smell might carry outside. We shouldn't use the lights either."

"That's fine," said Ginnie, her head in the well-stocked pantry. "Take a look at this." She stepped out of the way so that he could see the neat rows of canned goods that included fruit, tomatoes, and tuna. Further searching turned up half a loaf of bread, a hunk of cheese, and, finally, a can opener.

Some time later, Ginnie looked up from her plate. "I don't think I've ever eaten anything as good."

Damien pushed his chair back from the little kitchen table so that he could stretch his legs out. "I have to agree. A four-star restaurant couldn't have done better by us."

She studied him from beneath her lashes. He was wearing a pair of the jeans and one of the sports shirts they had bought together that day in California that now seemed so long ago. His appearance was a far cry from the man she had first seen on the terrace of Max's inn, always dressed in slacks and a white dress shirt, and then as he had been on the beach, dressed in a suit and dress shirt. He had always exuded overwhelming masculinity and sexuality. But now it seemed as though a transformation had taken place.

She had never seen him more alive, more vital. And it wasn't his clothing; she had seen him in the jeans before.

Their lives had taken a turn. Civilization was slowly fading away. Order, as they knew it, was disintegrating into chaos. They were now living on the edge, relying on fundamentals and primitive instinct. Every inch of Damien's six-foot one-inch frame was sizzlingly alive. And she had the feeling that she was seeing the *real* Damien Averone.

"This kitchen reminds me of my grandmother's," he said unexpectedly. "Did I ever mention her?"

"No. Tell me about her."

He lifted his leg and rested its ankle on the knee

of his other leg. "She was born and raised in Greece, but came to America as a young bride. Her husband, my grandfather, died when my father was a teenager. When I was growing up, she lived in a small apartment next door to ours, and she had spices hung in the corners of the kitchen, just like Julio's wife does here. My grandmother also had a crucifix over her stove like that one over there."

"Sounds like you have fond memories."

"She was a wonderful lady." He smiled reflectively. "She used to produce the most amazing meals on that old stove of hers." His smile broadened. "She also played the mandolin."

Her heart responded to the genuineness of his smile. Her mind tried to stay cool. "Really?"

He nodded. "Not wonderfully, like you play the guitar. But she picked out songs on it to amuse me. And she never once looked at me as if she didn't understand me."

In contrast to her, she thought regretfully. "I guess everyone needs at least one person in the world who accepts them completely," she said, her voice quiet and reflective. Then it came to her: Damien had been that person for her.

"Ginnie," he began. "I want you to know that I'm sorry for all the hurt I've caused you. I—" Sudden activity out on the road stopped him in midsentence. From the sound of it a large number of men were passing, both by car and on foot. He motioned her to stay where she was, got up, walked quietly to the window, and peered out the crack between the boards. After a moment he came back and sat down beside her. "Rebel troops," he whispered, taking her hand. "As long as we don't draw attention to ourselves, I don't think they'll bother us. They should be too busy right about now to be bothering with house-to-house searches. They'll be past in a minute."

With great determination she pushed her fear aside and nodded. Gripping his hand tightly, she tried to think of happy endings. She thought of Nathan, growing stronger day by day and eventually being able to fully enjoy his retirement. She thought of Michael, healthy and happy, back in San Francisco with his friends and his work and sometime in the future a fulfilling marriage with a woman who would love him as he deserved to be loved.

But most of all, in those moments when armed men were so near, she thought of her and Damien. Try as she might, though, she couldn't see a happy ending for them. They had loved each other so much, but somewhere along the line their love had gone wrong, and she didn't know if either of them knew how to make it right.

The noise of the rebel movement finally faded away, and Damien released her hand. But she found, somewhat disconcertedly, she wasn't ready for the disconnection. It had seemed right and natural to be comforting each other. His hand had been warm and strong over hers. She in turn had tried to be reassuring with her touch. And now . . .

For heaven's sake, Ginnie, you were just holding hands, not making a vow of love.

No, she thought, they had already said their vows. And beneath the night heavens, she had promised to "love, honor, and cherish, until death do us part."

She had always believed in honoring vows, not breaking them. She squeezed her eyes shut. *What had she done? What was she doing?* To cover her muddled feelings, she reached for her plate and started to rise.

He reached out and put his hand on her arm, a staying gesture. "Ginnie, there's something I want to say to you before it's too late."

"Too late?" She sank back to her chair. "I don't like the sound of that."

He rolled one shoulder, then the other, easing their tightness. "I meant only that once we get Michael and go back home, there probably won't be another opportunity for me to say this." He paused, collecting his thoughts. He didn't believe for a minute that what he was about to tell her would make a difference between them. No, he reflected, this confession would be for her, to tell her that she had been right after all and to make her feel better. It would also be for his own conscience, something that until recently he hadn't been sure he had.

"A few days ago in Nathan's office you accused me of sending Michael down here because I was jealous of him. I denied it. And I have to say I was being truthful"—he grimaced—"or rather as truthful as I was capable of being at the time. But since then I've done a lot of thinking, and I don't like what I've discovered." He absently rubbed his forehead. "The day in New York that I walked in and saw you and Michael together, I went a little crazy. He was a man who meant a lot to you, and I knew he was trying to get you away from me. I couldn't stand it. I felt more threatened than I ever had in my life."

"Good Lord, Damien. I was saying *good-bye* to him. That same night I became your *wife*."

He looked bleakly at her. "I know, but I didn't want to take any chances whatsoever. That's how frightened I was of losing you. When I called California to check on things that afternoon, I was advised about the situation down here. Without thinking twice, without considering the consequences, I told them to send Michael."

She didn't know what to think. "But you told me he was the best man for the job."

"He was, but looking back, I'm afraid that fact didn't play a very important part in my decision. I wanted him away from you."

"But why? Why were you so afraid of losing me? I loved you Damien. I had committed my life to you."

Past tense, he thought. She had used the past tense. The pain almost swamped him, taking with it energy and will and any slight hope that had remained. He felt like pleading with her, getting down on his knees and begging her to give them another chance, but she didn't deserve the burden of his needs. Not after the way he had hurt her. Now she deserved the truth.

"When we first met, I told you I didn't know how to have a relationship, and it was and is the truth. Around the time Max and I graduated from the Wharton School of Business, I fell in love with a girl." He smiled. "Or at least I thought it was love. I moved to New York, and she came with me. I remember being extremely happy. I had everything

I wanted, her and my new job. But I was just starting my career, and like all things I care passionately about, I became obsessed with it. Then one day I glanced around and she was gone. Knowing what I know now, I can't blame her, but at the time I was hurt." He rubbed his forehead again, wondering how he had suddenly become so tired, and reflecting that he hadn't known what hurting really was until he had lost Ginnie.

He forced himself to go on. "After that, there were other women. By then I was established, and I was aware that most of them were more interested in who I was than what I was, and I accepted it because none of them mattered to me." He smiled sadly. "Then I met you, and I got a first-class crash course in what *real* love is. And all I could think about was that I couldn't lose you. By then I was smart enough to know that love meant taking a risk. But with you I wanted to eliminate the risk. And that's what I tried to do, by any means possible."

"Is that why you didn't tell me about your buyout of Camden Electronics?"

"It was probably the root reason. But again, at the time I really didn't consider it important information. I've always been an expert at compartmentalizing my life. With you, I took it to extremes."

"I don't know what to say."

"There's nothing for you to say. I don't want to cause you one more moment of distress. I can only apologize from the bottom of my heart and promise you one more time that, no matter what it takes, I will get Michael and you safely out of this country." He hesitated, watching the pattern of conflicting emotions that crossed her face. "And, Ginnie . . . I would have come to get Michael whether you had come or not."

"I know that now."

"Good." He sighed heavily and rubbed his face. "I think I'll try to get some sleep."

He *did* look tired, she realized suddenly, as if he had been exhausted by what he had said. "Did you get any sleep last night?"

He shook his head and rose to his feet. "I'll stretch out on the couch."

She watched him leave the room but made no move to get up. A chain of thought had begun that wouldn't stop.

She remembered the last day in the States in Nathan's office when she had turned and walked out on Damien without waiting to find out what he would have said or done. And it was with a shock that she realized she had a history of walking away.

She had walked away from San Francisco instead of staying and making sure that Michael and Nathan *believed* her no. If she had stayed and made them believe her, Michael would never have come to New York to try and talk her into returning with him. Damien would never have gotten jealous. And so on and so on.

But she had left San Francisco. Then Damien had come along, and once again she had shunned responsibility by seeing herself as a victim.

But the truth was she had *allowed* him to sweep her off her feet, to the point that when Nathan had called and talked with her about his business problems, she hadn't really been that interested.

But the information had been there about the takeover. At any point, all she'd had to do was ask Nathan, or Michael, or even Damien.

But she'd been caught up in Damien as much as he'd been caught up in her.

All Damien had ever wanted was her, and everything he had done had been a means to that end. He had never expected anything of her except for her to love him. He had never set up a role or created a box and expected her to fill it. He had simply loved her for who she was. It was something she had known instinctively in the beginning, but somehow along the way had forgotten.

She'd cast him in the role of a villain, but he was a man, not always right, not always wrong. And in the end, though he had made some bad choices, it had been her own expectations that had hurt her, not someone else's.

Damien had only wanted her to be and to be his.

It took a while for the revelatory shock waves to subside. Then she rose and quietly cleaned up their meal.

He was already asleep by the time she returned to the living room. He lay on his back on the couch, one arm thrown over his head, the other across his waist. His breathing was even, his dark lashes lay in a semicircle over his beige-toned skin. But she sensed his guard remained in place even in sleep. There was a rifle leaning against the couch within arm's reach and a pistol on the coffee table beside him. Asleep or awake, he was trying to take care of her.

He had watched over her as she had slept last

night, she thought. She felt an inexpressible urge to do the same for him.

She retrieved a blanket from one of the bedrooms and lightly, tenderly spread it over him. Then she curled up in a chair in the corner and began her vigil.

The afternoon wore on. At one point she heard more troop movement out on the road. For a moment she considered waking Damien, but she quickly dismissed the idea. He needed his sleep; she'd wake him only if necessary. Now was her time to take care of him.

She reached for the rifle, eased over to a window, and made a quick check. With relief she saw a company of government troops, heading up into the hills. As soon as her heartbeat returned to normal, she replaced the rifle, leaning it against the couch as Damien had had it. And she took up her position in the chair and fixed her gaze on him.

She loved him. In fact, she had never stopped loving him.

Time passed, her heart grieved for the mistakes she had made, and eventually she grew drowsy and slept. Hours later when she awoke, the room was dark, and Damien wasn't on the couch.

Nine

"Damien?" Ginnie called softly. There was no answer. She called his name again as loud as she dared. There was still no answer.

With a trembling hand she lit a small candle and looked at her watch. *Eight-thirty.* Damien had left for his meeting with Zurdo and hadn't woken her to go with him! Dammit, she had planned to go with him. Now he was all alone.

When he had feared losing her, he had reverted to being the high-handed tycoon, using methods, both fair and unfair, to keep her . . . and now to keep her from harm. Even though she understood why he had gone to meet Zurdo alone, it made her furious. It also scared her to death.

She glanced at her watch again. The meeting wasn't until ten, but once Damien and Zurdo got there, it should take them no longer than five minutes to agree on a time and a place to deliver Michael. And, if she remembered the map correctly, it shouldn't take Damien more than thirty minutes to drive back to the house. Okay, she thought. By ten-thirty, eleven o'clock at the latest, Damien would be back. Until then she would stay busy. She would wash up, brush the rats out of her hair, maybe even change into a fresh pair of jeans and top. She would also prepare another meal out of cans and have it waiting for him. That's what she'd do, she decided, and prayed the time would pass fast.

At eleven o'clock Ginnie sat in the living room with every muscle tensed, the candle out, listening for the slightest sound of Damien. But all she could hear was guns. She jumped every time a new burst of gunfire exploded somewhere. She jumped a lot.

Why was he late? she wondered. Had something happened to him? They were surrounded by danger.

When another hour passed without any sign of him, she panicked. And by the time he climbed in the back window, two hours past the time she had mentally allotted him, she was almost incoherent with worry.

"Damien, good Lord, where have you been? What kept you? Are you all right?" She knelt beside the coffee table and lit the candle.

He dropped heavily onto the couch, and candlelight pooled over him and flickered on the wall behind him. "I'm fine. The meeting with Zurdo went off as planned. We'll pick up Michael at dawn in the morning in a clearing about an hour's drive up into the mountains. Only Zurdo and Michael are supposed to show up, all parties involved unarmed. I'll hand him the money, he'll give us Michael, and Max will fly in and pick us up."

"Fly in? In what?"

"If things on his end have gone according to plan, he's arranged for the use of a small helicopter for a few hours." He grinned. "American dollars at work."

Her adrenaline pumped to its top level, she rose and came around to sit beside him on the couch. Now they shared the pool of light, and she could see him more clearly. His face was dirty, and his shirt was torn. "You look awful! What happened? Were you hurt?"

"No, no, nothing like that. At one point my car got a flat, and I had to pull back into the woods and change the tire by Braille. I made pretty much a mess of it *and* myself, but I couldn't risk a light."

"Risk a light? What about risking your life? Lord, Damien, you're dumb!" She grabbed the candle and hurried away. In less than a minute she was back with a bowl of warm water and a cloth. "You're dumb, dumb, dumb," she said, washing his face none too gently. She was so close that his scent reached her, musky and hot. She grew angrier, and her eyes moistened with tears. "You knew very well that I intended to go with you, but you left without even waking me."

"That's right," he said, basking in the sensation of being nearer to her than he had been in days. Lord, he thought, but she was lovely. Thick, silky lashes surrounding deep, smoky eyes. A wide, passionate mouth that, at the moment, was turned down at the corners. Long, luxurious hair that somehow smelled of flowers and soap. His chest tightened. "Do you think you could leave me some skin, Ginnie?"

"No," she snapped.

He sighed. "Look, I fully admit that it was underhanded of me to leave the way I did, but I'm not going to apologize. If you'd been awake, you would have argued with me, and there was no way I wanted you with me. I would have been having to think about you as well as myself, and I had enough to worry about as it was."

She stopped scrubbing to glare at him. "So once again you manipulated things so that they would go your way."

"That's a fair interpretation."

She impatiently swatted at a tear that slid down her face and resumed the scrubbing. "And what was I supposed to do if something had happened to you?"

"You had food, water, and shelter here. Sooner or later government troops would have come by, and you could have asked for help to get to the airport."

"These people are fighting a war, Damien, not running a cab service."

"They would have helped you."

She was washing the same patch of skin over and over, she realized. She tossed the washcloth in the bowl and slumped back against the couch. "You thought of everything, didn't you?"

"I tried."

"Why were you gone so long?"

"A couple of times I had to pull off the road and drive into the woods to avoid some of the revolutionary forces."

"Dammit, Damien, they could have seen you!"

"Yeah, but they didn't. I drove slowly, without headlights, and with my head out the window so I could hear. And every so often I would stop and listen. Luckily, it worked."

But if it hadn't. Something seemed to come apart inside her. "You are so *dumb*," she whispered, "and I was so afraid."

He tried to smile, but failed. "I was too. I was afraid I'd never see you again."

She gave a soft cry and threw her arms around his neck, and was gratified when his arms came around her. She needed to feel the warmth of his skin to reassure herself that he was really all right. She needed to be held in his arms, to feel the passion rising inside her, to remind herself that there were emotions other than fear, and things that could happen other than the death and destruction going on in the city around them. She needed Damien.

She didn't want to feel empty and scared anymore. She didn't want to be without him one more minute. She wanted to feel the intoxication of their passion. She wanted to be able to remember that brief time when she had been loved by him, unconditionally and completely.

Her fingers slid up into his hair; she cradled his head with her hand and whispered in his ear. "Please . . ." Her breath feathered over his skin. "Make love to me."

He stiffened in surprise, but his hand smoothed up her back. "Are you sure?"

"Yes. *Please.*"

"Lord, Ginnie . . ."

Their clothes came off, clumsily, urgently. Naked, they lay back on the couch. Damien stroked his hand down her body, sucking in his breath at the sharp, jagged desire that cut through him. He could barely control himself—or her. His mouth covered hers, hot and hungry. He needed her so much. She opened herself for him, and he slid into her. And he groaned as he sheathed himself in the heated tightness of her. His muscles bunched and flexed as he drove in and out of her. She was a wild thing beneath him, straining up to meet him again and again. He couldn't control her; he couldn't control himself. It was a raw, primitive need that arrowed between them.

Guns blared in the distance. Fires burned around them.

They reached their first hard, powerful peak together, and the second, and the third.

The helicopter with Max at the controls settled at the edge of the mist-covered clearing.

Damien waved, then looked at Ginnie. "I'll get the money and be right back."

She nodded and watched him make his way toward the aircraft in a crouching run to minimize the blast of the air turbulence coming from the whirling rotors. He had been so quiet this morning, she reflected, and wished she knew what his thoughts were. What did he feel about what happened between them in the night? When he had awakened her to tell her to get ready, he was already dressed and with a preoccupied air about him. He hadn't spoken on the drive here either.

But she understood. It had taken total concentration on his part to maneuver up the treacherous mountain road.

Still, if he had just given some indication that he still loved her . . .

The mist carried a chill with it. She wrapped her arms around herself as she saw him take a canvas backpack from Max and start back to her. She wanted to tell him how much last night had meant to her. She wanted to tell him how much she loved him. And she would, she vowed, as soon as the two of them and Michael were safely out of this mess.

He returned to her side, the canvas backpack in his hand, just as she saw Zurdo and Michael break free of the mist.

Relief surged through her. Then her breath caught in her throat.

Michael was hurt.

He was limping and leaning heavily against the colonel with his arm around his neck. His other arm hung awkwardly at his side.

"Oh, Lord," she murmured. Wanting, needing, to help him, she took a step toward him.

Damien put a hand on her arm. "No, we've got to let them come to us."

She knew he was right, but she couldn't stop a cry of frustration escaping from her lips. As Michael drew closer, she could see that he was deathly pale and barely able to put one foot in front of the other. There was also a large clot of blood at his left temple.

Without waiting for word from either Zurdo or Damien, she reached for him. "Lord, Michael, what have they done to you?"

A spasm of pain stopped his attempt at a grin. "I was their . . . entertainment."

He fell against her, and she staggered. Damien stepped in, relieving her of most of Michael's weight.

Damien's face was grim. "I'm sorry, Michael. This is all my fault."

Michael's brow wrinkled in silent question.

"I sent you here."

Michael tried to laugh, but the laughter turned to a choke. "I wanted to come. I . . . volunteered before you ever came. . . ." He reeled, but Damien was able to catch him.

Ginnie's eyes briefly closed as she remembered the telephone conversation she had had with Nathan. He had said, "*Michael is chomping at the bit to go. . . .*" Would things have been any different between her and Damien now if she had remembered that conversation sooner? She had so many regrets.

"I thought . . . I could . . . help," Michael said, each word an effort.

"This is all very nice, I'm sure," said Zurdo, a sneer on his face, his eyes flat, "but I would like my money now."

Damien hurled the pack at him. "You're a sonofabitch, Zurdo. My only consolation is that you won't live long enough to spend this money. One side or the other is going to kill you."

The colonel's lips pulled back from his teeth in an eerie smile. "It is a popular myth that right always prevails, Señor Averone. *Adios.*"

"Let's get out of here," Damien muttered. "The

hairs on the back of my neck are standing straight up, and I don't like the feeling."

Ginnie struggled with her share of Michael's weight as they headed toward the waiting helicopter. The sight of the whirling rotors kept her moving forward, even though his occasional groans of pain wrenched her heart. "There's a jet waiting at the airport, Michael. We'll be back in San Francisco by tonight."

"Yeah," Damien interjected, "and I'm going to see to it that you get the best possible care."

"I hope that care"—Michael took a ragged gulp of air—"includes several pain pills and a clean bed. . . ."

"Anything you want—"

Suddenly, gunfire broke the early morning silence of the clearing. Ginnie glanced over her shoulder. Through the mist she could just make out men streaming out of the woods on the far side of the clearing, their guns blazing.

"Run!" Damien took Michael's full weight, half-dragging him, half-carrying him.

Ginnie reached the helicopter a few feet ahead of Damien and Michael. Max had the door open, ready for them. His big body tensed over the controls, his gaze was fixed on the two men coming behind her. She turned just as Damien released Michael to her.

"Get him in the copter," he said tersely, his teeth gritted. That's when she saw blood soaking through Damien's shirt and spreading over his shoulder.

"You've been *shot!*"

"I'm all right." He reached into the helicopter

and grabbed an automatic rifle, exchanging a look with Max as he did.

"Damien—"

"Dammit, get Michael in! I'll cover you until you do."

"Damien, watch out," Max yelled.

He whirled just in time to see Zurdo hurling himself at him. Damien caught him, and they fell to the ground.

Over their struggling bodies Ginnie could see rebels advancing. Desperate, tears streaming down her face, Ginnie pushed Michael, causing him to fall into the open doorway of the helicopter. Then she scrambled over him, braced her feet against the seat legs, and pulled. By the time she had gotten him in, he had lapsed into unconsciousness.

When she looked up again, Zurdo was on top of Damien and had just connected a fist to Damien's face. "Help him, Max!"

Pale, his jaw fiercely set, Max didn't move. "I can't leave the controls."

Ginnie's heart was in her throat as she watched the two men in their life-and-death fight. "A gun! Max, where's a gun?"

"A gun's no good. If you shoot at Zurdo, you're going to hit Damien."

On the ground, Damien slugged Zurdo. At the same time he managed to yell, "Take off!"

"No! Max, we're not leaving him!"

"Dammit," Damien yelled again, "*take off*!"

Max cursed and checked the rebels. "Another minute and they're going to be right on top of us.

We've got to get out of here or we're going to be blown to smithereens."

"You can't leave him!"

"I have my orders." Max lifted the helicopter off the ground, his face a mask of anguish.

"*Damien, I love you!*" The scream came from Ginnie's soul.

"Is there any news?" Ginnie asked anxiously when Michael called her as he did now each evening. They had been back in the States a little over a week. He had discharged himself from the hospital after only a three-day stay. And ever since, he had been working to find out what he could about Damien.

"I'm sorry, honey, no. There hasn't been any word."

"You didn't hear from Max?" Several days before, Max had flown back to Sagrado Montanas to initiate a new search, but as the days had passed without any promising word, her hope had faded.

"No, but you know that doesn't mean anything."

"Thank you for trying to make me feel better."

"No, I mean it. Even though the government is back in control, I can't always get through on the telephone. Unfortunately, a lot of destruction has taken place, and it's still pretty much chaos down there."

"But the government *is* helping, aren't they?"

"Oh, yes, they've been very willing to do whatever they can. Remember, they're going to need financial aid now, more than ever. Anyway, Max gave them the exact coordinates of that clearing, and they've sent out scouting patrols."

"But they haven't found Damien." Her tone was flat.

"You can't give up, honey. Zurdo is a greedy bastard, and Damien is too valuable for him to kill."

"But we haven't received any ransom note."

"That doesn't necessarily mean we won't."

"It doesn't mean we will either."

Michael sighed. "I guess it all depends on what's happened to Zurdo. Looking back, he concocted that little surprise party in the first place because he not only wanted the two hundred thousand, he also wanted the supposed fortune a ransom for me, you, and Damien combined would bring."

Ginnie fell quiet. Michael had been wonderful, but there was a lot he wasn't saying. He thought Damien was dead. By rights, she supposed she should be thinking the same thing. But she couldn't. . . . She couldn't. . . . She finally asked, "How are you doing?"

"I'm fine, honey. Don't worry about me. You just take care of yourself, and I'll call you if I hear anything."

If. "Thank you, Michael. Good-bye."

An hour later, her guitar in hand, Ginnie walked listlessly along the beach toward the rock where she had sat every evening since she had come back.

Damien couldn't be dead. She refused even to contemplate the thought. Because if she did, it would mean Damien had given his life to save her and Michael. It would also mean he had died thinking she didn't love him.

The whole idea was intolerable to her. Awake or asleep, she spent all her energy fighting against believing he was dead. But beneath the surface of her bravado, a cold, jagged fear nagged her constantly, fear that she would never see him again.

Even though the sun had long since set, the sand still retained the warmth of the day and felt warm beneath her bare feet. It was a feeling she noticed only absently, as she did most things lately.

She spent the greater part of each day in San Francisco with Nathan, who, thankfully, was well on the road to complete recovery. By late afternoon she was back at her houseboat. There, she would spend a few hours tending her flowers, Michael would call, and then she would take her walk.

And remember. She would remember Damien, his rugged face, his voice of silk and granite, his astonishing smile. She would remember their time together, the fun times, the passionate times. And most of all, she would remember how much she loved him.

During the day she managed to contain her feelings. But in the evening they all came out—in her music.

She settled onto the rock and pulled her guitar close to her. And she began to play, play out her grief, her regret, her love.

The music flowed from her, out into the night, over the sea, down the beach, and to the barefoot man dressed in jeans and a sweater who had come up while she played. . . .

He listened, devouring the sight and sound of her, filling his senses with the vision she made, her hair waving about her head and shoulders, her slim body bent over the guitar, her long legs encased in her favorite jeans. And he waited until the last note had died away. "I don't think I've ever heard anything more beautiful," he said huskily.

Her head snapped up, and her eyes widened in disbelief.

"And I know I've never seen anything as beautiful as you." A smile of tenderness curved his lips, but his fist was clenched. And inside he was terrified that no matter what she had said when the helicopter had lifted off, she wouldn't accept him back.

"Damien." She whispered his name on a soft breath, afraid to say the name too loud for fear he would disappear.

"It's me."

Dropping the guitar, she launched herself off the rock and into his arms. *"Damien!"*

With only the slightest of grimaces, he caught her against him. Tears burned at his eyes. Closing them, he absorbed the scent of her perfume and the softness of her curves. There had been many times in the last two weeks when he had been fearful he would never hold her again.

"Lord, Damien, I've been so afraid you were—" She couldn't even say the words.

"I heard you tell me you loved me. After that, nothing could have kept me away from you."

"Damien . . ." Her eyes welled with tears, and

she ran her hands over his face, touching him as much as she could, the feel of him on her fingertips reassuring her he was real. "But how—?"

"Max found me today and flew me home."

"Thank God!" A sob broke from her, but it was a sob of happiness. She wrapped her arms tightly around his neck, then abruptly pulled back as she felt the padding of a thick bandage beneath the sweater. "Your shoulder!"

"It's going to be fine. By the time I managed to make it to the hospital, it was pretty infected, but they got the bullet out and started me on antibiotics."

"But what happened? How did you even get to a hospital? When we took off, Zurdo was on top of you, and the rebels were closing in."

"I was able to overcome Zurdo, retrieve the rifle, and drag him into the woods before the rebels got to us."

"Max circled the clearing several times, trying to keep you in sight, but the mist obscured everything, and the gunfire became too dangerous."

"I know. I heard the copter, but Max did exactly what he was supposed to by taking off. We had already discussed all contingencies."

She shook her head, trying to rid herself of the memory of that awful moment when they had flown off to safety and left him. "I still have nightmares about us leaving you. I gave Max an awful time."

He grinned. "Yeah, that's what he said. He also said he was afraid to come home without me for fear of what you'd do to him."

"Actually, Max has been great. I was pretty hysterical and Michael was unconscious, but he got us out of there. What happened to Zurdo?"

"The mist was really thick in the woods and helped hide us. I kept him with me until I didn't need him as a shield anymore, then I knocked him unconscious, grabbed up the money, and got away. But it took me several days to make it back to the city, and the first person I saw shoved me into the hospital. Things were confused, but they took care of me."

"Thank heavens." Fine tremors shook her body, tension fading, relief rising. "And now you're here."

"Now I'm here."

Needing to maintain contact with him, she lightly smoothed her hand across the shoulder that wasn't hurt. "Damien, can you ever forgive me?"

He started with surprise. "Forgive you for *what*? I was the one who made the mistakes."

She gave a short, rueful laugh. "I made mistakes too. A *lot* of them. But I never stopped loving you. I couldn't. I love you too much."

He groaned as emotion shuddered hard through his body. "It was that thought that kept me going, that and the hope that we could start a new life together. Can we, Ginnie?"

In the light of the moon her face glowed with joy. "It's what I want most in the world."

He couldn't wait a moment longer. His mouth fastened hungrily on hers while his hands slid over her, rediscovering her. She tasted like everything he'd ever been hungry for, she felt like everything he'd ever wanted. He had come so close to losing her, he thought, still shaken by the idea, but he was wiser now. His love had grown deeper, more mature, and even more powerful. He broke off the kiss and looked down at her, cradling her face between his big hands. "We're going to make it this time, Ginnie."

"Yes," she agreed simply, but with her whole heart.

He picked up her guitar and held out his hand. "Let's go home."

"Home?" she asked, momentarily confused about where he meant. "Where?"

"The houseboat."

THE EDITOR'S CORNER

For the best in summertime reading, look no further than the six superb LOVESWEPTs coming your way. As temperatures soar, what better way is there to escape from it all than by enjoying these upcoming love stories?

Barbara Boswell's newest LOVESWEPT is guaranteed to sweep you away into the marvelous world of high romance. A hell raiser from the wrong side of the tracks, Caleb Strong is back, and no red-blooded woman can blame Cheyenne Whitney Merit for giving in to his STRONG TEMPTATION, LOVESWEPT #486. The bad boy who left town years ago has grown into one virile hunk, and his hot, hungry kisses make "good girl" Cheyenne go wild with longing. But just as Caleb burns with desire for Cheyenne, so is he consumed by the need for revenge. And only her tender, healing love can drive away the darkness that threatens their fragile bond. A dramatic, thrilling story that's sensuously charged with unlimited passion.

The hero and heroine in SIZZLE by Marcia Evanick, LOVESWEPT #487, make the most unlikely couple you'll ever meet, but as Eben James and Summer Hudson find out, differences add spice to life . . . and love. Eben keeps his feet firmly planted in the ground, so when he discovers his golden-haired neighbor believes in a legendary sea monster, he's sure the gods are playing a joke on him. But there's nothing laughable about the excitement that crackles on the air whenever their gazes meet. Throwing caution to the wind, he woos Summer, and their courtship, at once uproarious and touching, will have you believing in the sheer magic of romance.

Welcome back Joan J. Domning, who presents the stormy tale of love lost, then regained, in RAINY DAY MAN, LOVESWEPT #488. Shane Halloran was trouble with a capital *T* when Merle Pierce fell hard for him in high school, but she never believed the sexy daredevil would abandon her. She devoted herself to her teenage advice column and tried to forget the man who ruined her for others. Now, more than twenty years later, fate intervenes, and Shane learns a truth Merle would have done anything to hide from him. Tempers flare but are doused in the sea of their long-suppressed passion for each other. Rest assured that all is forgiven between these two when the happy ending comes!

With her spellbinding sensuality, well-loved author Helen Mittermeyer captures A MOMENT IN TIME, LOVESWEPT #489. Hawk Dyhart acts like the consummate hero when he bravely rushes into the ocean to save a swimmer from a shark. Never mind that the shark turns out to be a diving flag and the swimmer an astonishingly beautiful woman who's furious at being rescued. Bahira Massoud is a magnificently exotic creature that Hawk must possess, but Bahira knows too well the danger of surrendering to a master of seduction. Still, she aches to taste the desire that Hawk arouses in her, and Hawk must walk a fine line to capture this sea goddess in his arms. Stunning and breathtaking, this is a romance you can't let yourself miss.

Let Victoria Leigh tantalize you with LITTLE SECRETS, LOVESWEPT #490. Ex-spy turned successful novelist I. J. Carlson drives Cassandra Lockland mad with his mocking glances and wicked come-ons. How could she be attracted to a man who provokes her each time they meet? Carlson sees the fire beneath her cool facade and stokes it with kisses that transform the love scenes in his books into sizzling reality. Once he breaches her defenses and uncovers her hidden fears, he sets out on a glorious campaign to win her trust. Will she be brave enough to face the risk of loving again? You'll be thoroughly mesmerized by this gem of a book.

Mary Kay McComas certainly lands her hero and heroine in a comedy of errors in ASKING FOR TROUBLE, LOVESWEPT #491. It all starts when Sydney Wiesman chooses Tom Ghorman from the contestants offered by the television show *Electra-Love*. He's smart, romantic, funny—the perfect man for the perfect date—but their evening together is filled with one disaster after another. Tom courageously sees them through each time trouble intervenes, but he knows this woman of his dreams can never accept the one thing in his life he can't change. Sydney must leave the safe and boring path to find the greatest adventure of all—a future with Tom. Don't miss this delectable treat.

FANFARE presents four truly spectacular books in women's popular fiction next month. Ask your bookseller for TEXAS! CHASE, the next sizzling novel in the TEXAS! trilogy by bestselling author Sandra Brown, THE MATCHMAKER by critically acclaimed Kay Hooper, RAINBOW by the very talented Patricia Potter, and FOLLOW THE SUN by ever-popular Deborah Smith.

Enjoy the summer with perfect reading from LOVESWEPT and FANFARE!

With every good wish,

Carolyn Nichols

Carolyn Nichols
Editor
LOVESWEPT
Bantam Books
666 Fifth Avenue
New York, NY 10103

60 Minutes to a Better, More Beautiful You!

Now it's easier than ever to awaken your sensuality, stay slim forever—even make yourself irresistible. With Bantam's bestselling subliminal audio tapes, you're only 60 minutes away from a better, more beautiful you!

__ 45004-2	**Slim Forever**	$8.95
__ 45035-2	**Stop Smoking Forever**	$8.95
__ 45022-0	**Positively Change Your Life** ...	$8.95
__ 45041-7	**Stress Free Forever**	$8.95
__ 45106-5	**Get a Good Night's Sleep**	$7.95
__ 45094-8	**Improve Your Concentration** .	$7.95
__ 45172-3	**Develop A Perfect Memory**	$8.95

NEW!

Handsome Book Covers Specially Designed To Fit Loveswept Books

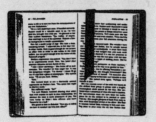

Our new French Calf Vinyl book covers come in a set of three great colors—royal blue, scarlet red and kachina green.

Each 7" × 9½" book cover has two deep vertical pockets, a handy sewn-in bookmark, and is soil and scratch resistant.

To order your set, use the form below.